Symposium of the Reaper

Volume 2

SYMPOSIUM OF THE REAPER: VOLUME 2

Andrew Adams

ISBN (Print Edition): 978-1-66787-967-3

ISBN (eBook Edition): 978-1-66787-968-0

Contents

XIV

The Hunger...
It Aches

"Are you certain this is the right place? Seems a bit too…quaint."

"This is the address, Dorothy. He also gave me specific directions and said we couldn't miss it."

"Really, Danny, you should be more careful about mingling with strangers. What type of person invites someone over for supper after having just met them?"

"But Dorothy, you were the one that wanted to meet new people in the area, right?"

"Yeah, well…goodness, this is just a bit different than what we are used to, that's all."

"That's what happens when you move from the city to a small town," Danny grins. "There is bound to be an adjustment period, and I'm sure having a new friend will assist with that."

"Maybe you're right, I will try to keep an open mind. What is his name again?"

"Eugene. He's a great chef, as well. He told me so when we met at the market."

"I sure am hungry," Dorothy admits, lightly touching her stomach. "I wonder how far away the next closest house is from here?"

Dorothy continues walking gingerly down the dirt path, scanning the surrounding environment of crooked trees and misleading shadows. The wind blows lightly with an atmospheric whistle.

"I'm excited, are you? You're going to love him, I'm sure of it!" Danny enthuses.

"Is that his food I smell cooking? Wow..." Dorothy stutter steps with her nose in the air, more excited over the prospect of finally eating than meeting Eugene. "I'm sure he's very nice."

"Oh, he is. That must be the cottage right there," Danny points, picking up the pace in anticipation. "Do you want to knock, or should I?"

"I...don't care either way. You go ahead, he is your friend after all."

"Yes, but after dinner, he is going to be OUR friend. Gosh, living in a small town is going to be so great for us."

Danny grins a bit too wide as he turns to knock on the door. He raps his knuckles three times on the wood as they both stand back with bated breath. Dorothy swallows hard, staring at the foreboding door apprehensively.

"Danny, welcome!" Eugene greets as he swings the door inward, placing a hand on Danny's shoulder. "And you must be Dorothy! Beautiful, just as described. Please, come in! Come in, come in, there are creatures out there just waiting to pounce. I kid, but really, let us get inside."

"That is very kind, Eugene. You have a beautiful home and we can't thank you enough for welcoming us," Dorothy offers.

"Nonsense, just having you here is entirely my pleasure. I understand it must have been quite the trek for you both, so allow me to act as your servant for the evening. Host duties and the like, and I'm afraid I must insist."

"Thank you. I couldn't help but notice the wonderful smell of food cooking as we approached your house. May I ask what we are having tonight?"

"Well…" Eugene grins, "I typically prefer to keep that a surprise, but I will just say it is a stew, of sorts. No more telling!"

"It smells delicious, Eugene," Danny interjects. "I'm not much of a cook, so I bet you Dorothy is just dying to eat a home cooked meal she didn't have to slave over." His laughter is saccharine.

"Do you enjoy beef stew, Dorothy?"

"Oh, goodness me, I do," she salivates.

"Splendid. I am sure you will love your meal, in that case. Forgive my manners! Allow me to take your coats." Eugene grabs their clothing garments and lays them nonchalantly over the back of the sofa. "Sit, please."

Dorothy flashes a meek grin and sits back against her coat, grimacing at the wrinkles she will have to iron out later. Danny plops down with a large, fascinated grin.

"Eugene, I wanted Dorothy to be caught up by the time we arrived, so I told her all about you on our way here."

"Good things, I hope! Only in jest, Dorothy," Eugene winks at her. "Danny also told me quite a bit about you at the market. I couldn't wait to meet you."

"Yes, umm…likewise. I am very happy to be here. We just moved into town and it is always comforting to make new friends. Danny and I move often for work."

"You know, Danny, in our very long conversation and all the things we discussed, I do not believe you ever told me what it is you do?"

"I-"

"Hold that thought for just a moment, I believe my egg timer is going off. Allow me to go check on the food and then we can continue from there."

Eugene scurries into the kitchen through the saloon-style door. Dorothy slowly swivels her head to stare directly at Danny.

"What is it, dear?"

"I didn't hear an egg timer…he's very-"

"Isn't he great? I can't wait to come over here for dinner all the time! What do you think, maybe every Saturday night? Friday AND Saturday?" Danny lights up.

"Won't that decision be at least partially up to him?"

"I need to learn how to cook! I can make the three of us supper just like we're having here! Luckily, I know a great cook who can teach me."

"Are you also going to cook for me if Eugene isn't around?" Dorothy mocks.

Danny sits perplexed, as if the thought had never crossed his mind.

"But…you cook, so why would I also make food?"

Eugene bursts through the swinging kitchen door like a tornado, beaming and holding a washcloth tightly around his left hand.

"Not ready quite yet, but I can assure you, it is delicious! Couldn't help myself, I had to take a sample. Naughty me, naughty indeed."

"Is everything okay, Eugene? You're bleeding," Dorothy notices with genuine concern.

"Oh, you mean this? Just a scratch, that's all."

Eugene adjusts his makeshift bandage, accidentally dropping it on the table with a sodden plop. Danny is too pre-occupied to notice, reveling in his surroundings.

"Eugene…that's a LOT of blood, let me help you. Did you accidentally cut off your fingertip?"

He spreads his fingers apart and quickly gives them a flutter.

"This? No, that happened long ago, however I opened the wound once again with a cheese grater. Clumsy me!" he chuckles, covering his hand again.

"He's fine, dear. Don't be rude, it's unbecoming to bring attention to a deformity. No offense, Eugene."

But Dorothy is not as easily fooled as Danny, for on his other three fingers, Eugene is missing a knuckle or two as well. She is shocked that she did not notice this before.

"None taken, Danny. You're too kind, Dorothy. I am perfectly fine, and immensely enjoying the company this evening."

Blood drips from the washcloth onto the table, seemingly in conjunction with the grandfather clock beside them.

"Eugene, Dorothy and I were thinking it might be fun to do this every weekend?" Danny bubbles over. Dorothy is mortified.

"That WOULD be fun, although maybe we should see how the night goes first," Eugene replies, grinning. "Pardon me, just a moment."

Dorothy glares at Danny across the table as Eugene dashes back into the kitchen.

"You didn't tell me he was missing most of a hand!" she chastises under her breath.

"I...I guess I didn't notice at the market. We were talking so much, I didn't look at his fingers. What does it matter, anyway?"

"I could have not embarrassed myself had I known, Danny!"

"You're fine, honey. He doesn't seem upset in the slightest."

Eugene bursts through the door once again, frightening Dorothy and causing her to jump up and spin around to look behind her. She catches a glimpse of the kitchen each time the door swings back and forth like a pendulum. A gargantuan black cauldron hangs in a wood burning fireplace. How incredibly odd the countryside is.

"Nosy, nosy! Trying to steal a peek at your supper?" he teases. Eugene is now wearing a coat while carrying a tray with one hand. He places it down on the table gently and hands a wine glass to both Danny and Dorothy before taking his own, which is nearly overflowing. The left arm of the coat appears to be hanging entirely limp.

"To new friends!" Danny toasts, raising his glass.

"To friends," Eugene echoes, downing his entire cup of wine in one go. "Ah, delicious! What's the matter, Dorothy? Don't you like wine?"

"I do, but unfortunately I don't tolerate it very well, so I just have to take my time. It is very tasty, though."

"She's a bit of a lightweight, Eugene."

"Thanks for clarifying, Danny. Take all the time you need, my dear. After all, we are here for pleasure, are we not? No need to stress yourself on my account."

Eugene turns behind him and grabs an open bottle of wine, pouring another massive glass and gulping it down as if it is set to expire.

"I will take a refill, as well!" Danny exclaims, copying Eugene and cascading the wine down his throat.

"Really, Danny, you should pace yourself. You wouldn't want to get too sauced and not be able to take Dorothy home, right? Here, have another glass."

"Thank you, just one more for me in that case."

"Cheers," Eugene wishes him as he pours another. "We wouldn't want you going thirsty, either, not under my roof. Dinner is ALMOST done, just sit tight."

And with that, he vanishes as quickly as he ran into the room.

"Danny, I don't know how I feel about this anymore. Did you SEE his arm? It's gone!"

"And where could it possibly have gone, Dorothy? Maybe he was cold and had it tucked inside his coat?"

"Doesn't that just seem a bit strange like everything else so far tonight?" she pleads. "Why would he carry a tray of drinks with one hand while the other is tucked inside his shirt? I don't like this."

"You've lived in the city too long, sweetheart. The bright lights and taxi cabs have made you a distrusting person, but I have a feeling you will warm up to the country soon enough. I know I already am," he boasts, sipping wine.

Dorothy rolls her eyes in disdain, knowing in her gut that something isn't right. The food, however, smells absolutely wonderful...the one sip of wine she took has her stomach grumbling even more than before. Perhaps it wouldn't be horrible to at least sample the meal...

Ten minutes pass, then twenty, as Danny and Dorothy sit quietly at the table waiting for Eugene to return. Danny finished his glass of wine and snuck another from the bottle Eugene kept hidden in plain sight on the shelf.

"Dinner is served! My sincerest apologies for the wait, but nothing good comes quickly. Here we have a plate of cheeses to pair with your wine. Dorothy, you didn't finish your glass!"

"Yes, I mean no...I was waiting for my supper."

"Here's your supper. Finish your wine first."

Dorothy looks around uncomfortably and decides to down the rest of the glass. One quick course of dinner then they can be on their way. No use in arguing now.

"There. What are we eating?" she asks in return.

"As I said, a cheese plate for starters. Dig in," he says, pouring another cup for Dorothy. "I will bring in the second and third courses now." Eugene turns to walk away, but is obviously limping with a crutch under his arm and Dorothy sees it clear as day.

"Um, Eugene?"

"Yes, my dear Dorothy?" He turns to face her.

"Are you alright? You're limping now."

Eugene's pant leg seems to be as hollow as his shirt sleeve, although with nowhere else to stuff the limb, as could be the case with his arm.

"It looks like your leg is missing?" Dorothy questions incredulously.

"I have always been this way, Dorothy, nothing is wrong. Quite the opposite, really," he beams, downing another glass of wine.

"Danny? Anything?"

Danny looks back and forth between Dorothy and Eugene's missing leg contemplatively. "I would love another glass of wine!"

"Oh, alright, you big oaf. Knock yourself out."

Eugene fills Danny's glass to the brim as Dorothy's panic begins to crescendo. Her eyes dart around the room frantically seeking answers, yet finding nothing. A warming sensation crawls outward from her core, blanketing her limbs with a gentle tingle.

"I apologize, Eugene. Who am I to judge?"

"Nobody, but I forgive you nonetheless," he soothes, kissing her on the top of the head. "Now, please, let's enjoy dinner. I will be right out with the main course."

Eugene grabs a piece of cheese and tosses the entire thing in his mouth, followed by his guests doing the same. He backs through the swinging door and disappears.

"Danny…this cheese is delicious!" Dorothy proclaims, grabbing several more pieces and chomping down.

"Agreed, this is the best cheese I have ever had! Good old country comfort."

"Here we are! The main course, my special stew!" Eugene announces.

"That sounds great, Eugene, but do you have any more cheese?" Dorothy inquires.

"Yes! The cheese!" Danny echoes.

"You ate it all? Better have more wine then to wash it down. I'm afraid that won't be possible. I don't have any more cheese made yet."

They both groan.

"What will it take to get more? How did you make it?" Danny asks.

"Essentially, I grew it. I don't have any more prepared."

"You GREW it?" Dorothy scoffs.

"Drink your wine, hurry. But yes, I grew it. Those slices of cheese were taken from my skin. I suppose it isn't actually cheese without dairy, but that is the easiest way to refer to it in simple terms. I don't have any more skin available to make you more."

"Oh. That makes sense."

"Never had a better slice of real cheese, Eugene," Danny brown-noses.

"Splendorous," Eugene mutters as he grabs two more full goblets of wine. "Drink. You need to try the stew, but drink first."

The lovely couple both chug their wine like parched desert wanderers who finally found water.

"Stew, please," Dorothy demands.

"I can't wait for the stew," Danny follows.

Eugene sets his tray down and carefully hands out bowls of soup with one hand, although it now has only three fingers. Dorothy stares at him, bewildered.

"Something to say, my dear?"

"Yes, I'm starving!"

"Excellent," Eugene soothes. "This is my favorite meal. Eugene stew, or if you will, Stewgene. Enjoy." He grabs a third bowl from behind and dives in, slurping and munching noisily.

"This is scrumptious!" Danny compliments.

"Yes, very good," Dorothy agrees, biting into something crunchy.

All three of them guzzle and swallow like pigs in slop.

"This is amazing! Do you happen to have any more carrots? It's my favorite food," she blushes.

Eugene, never one to be rude, keeps his mouth shut while it is full of food and nods instead. He fishes his ring finger from his soup and drops it on the table cloth, chopping it into more reasonably-sized bites of carrot before scooping them up and sprinkling them over Dorothy's bowl.

"Thank you so much," she says, crunching into the finger slice.

"Dorothy loves carrots, but I'm all about the meat. What is it? It's tender and delicious."

"My thigh, mostly. Perhaps a bit of calf."

"Incredible."

Eugene beams in approval while gobbling his own bowl and stabbing a small cocktail fork into his left index finger. "I prefer my carrots whole," he notes as he tosses the entire digit into his mouth.

Dorothy and Danny nod in acknowledgement.

"More wine?" Eugene offers.

"Yes."

"Please."

"Save some room for desert, you two. I had quite a bit of leftover meat, so I made pies and tossed the rest in to the stew pot."

Yet the couple gorges still.

Eugene rips apart a hearty piece of meat, satisfied at how everything this evening has gone so well. Nights like this don't come along often.

"There's a fingernail on my carrot," Dorothy announces.

"Don't be shy, just spit it out in your napkin. I'll get it later."

"Here, honey. Take some of my carrots, I have a ton." Danny drops a few pieces into her bowl.

Dorothy stares into her stew blankly, then looks back and forth from man to man.

"How is your Stewgene? Is everything satisfactory?"

"Are you okay, Dorothy?" Danny asks.

Dorothy continues to stare in confusion. After a brief moment, her head crashes down, catching the edge of her soup bowl and launching it across the table.

"Danny…Danny, wake up."

Danny stirs, hearing his name from a distant and murky source. Where is he?

"Danny, have some stew. It will help you feel better. Sit up."

He forces his eyes open and sits up in discomfort, looking around the room yet nothing makes sense. Eugene stares at him eye to eye, standing on his hip nubs. All that remains of him now is a patchwork torso and right arm with two fingers.

"I already ate my soup."

"That was last night, Danny. It will be sunrise before too long and you are hungry again, I know you are. Eat." Eugene rubs his cheek with his three finger stubs.

"Yeah, well…the soup WAS mighty delicious."

"I'm afraid we ran out of Stewgene and there won't be any more. You will absolutely love my new batch. Try it. Here, I will even feed it to you."

Eugene fills the spoon with soup and gently pushes it between Danny's lips to guide it down his throat, as if feeding a convalescent.

"There we go, much better," Eugene whispers.

Danny's eyes open wide with sudden clarity. The second soup is even better than the first.

"Give me that," he demands, "I can feed myself." Danny yanks the bowl away from Eugene and ravenously slurps, gulps, and guzzles the stew in whatever manner can transport it to his stomach in the quickest way possible. "Wine, please."

"No more wine. We need you to sober up."

Danny eyes him, yet can't afford to waste time away from his bowl. Finally, he sets it down next to him with a clink from the metal spoon on the porcelain dish.

"That was…incredible. I need more."

"You can have it all. That entire pot is yours, I have no use for it."

"How could a stew be so tasty and fulfilling? So pleasurable to eat? Tell me what is in it!" Danny implores.

"I call it Dorothy Bisque."

"Oh."

"Yes?" Eugene leans in closer.

"I was wondering where she went."

"Yes, well she is within you now, as am I and others before within me."

Danny stares at him blankly.

"The wine, Danny. Drugged, I'm afraid, to impose an extremely docile and obedient sense of complacency. The wine you drank tonight, as well as the bottle I gifted you at the market were both drugged, although apparently only you partook, not Dorothy."

"She doesn't really drink. She's a lightweight, remember?"

"But of course," Eugene says, plopping himself on Danny's lap. "You, my friend, drank so much wine I doubt the drugs have even had time to wear off yet. Enjoy it while it lasts."

"Enjoy what?"

"The feeling of the drugs, or lack thereof. Once they wear off, you will be in excruciating agony unlike anything you ever thought possible. You ate your new bride, Danny. Slurped her from the rim of a soup bowl."

"She was delectable," Danny nods in monotone.

"Yes, she was. What will you do when you have no more? Even in your current state, I'm sure you can imagine there will never be another batch of Dorothy Bisque again."

Danny's face drops.

"You will hunger for that taste and know it will never come. As the drugs wear off, you will feel the unbearable weight of grief, and the more you miss her, the more you will crave the flavor until the two become synonymous. Only then will you feel the pain I once felt. The type of misery to never subside under any circumstances, no matter what you do, even though you will try to alleviate it."

"That sounds awful. No more Dorothy Bisque?" Danny droops.

"No. No more, ever again, unless…no, you probably wouldn't want to do that. Forget I said anything."

"Tell me! I will do anything!"

"Well…" Eugene smirks, "once the pot of Dorothy Bisque has been eaten, there will be ONE source remaining, but only one for the rest of time."

"TELL ME!"

"It's you, Danny. Dorothy exists within you now, and that will be the only opportunity for the rest of your life, so act quickly! But, remember your manners and never feast alone. You will need to find guests, as I did and others before me have done."

"You mean like Dorothy and me?"

"Very good, Danny." Eugene reaches up to stroke Danny's face with his remaining fingers. "You were my dinner guests as I was a guest before in this very house. Those are the rules, you can only get to Dorothy once you have another couple over for dinner. We must always follow hosting etiquette no matter how bad the hunger grows to be."

Danny stares into the eyes of the half-man standing on his lap. The question 'why?' floats through his brain, then travels on down the river of thought as quickly as it appeared.

"Is there any more wine?" he utters.

"Enough to drown yourself in, my boy. In the wine cellar, you will find everything you need. Take care, Danny. It was a pleasure having you over to eat me."

Eugene hobbles across the floor to the giant cauldron full of boiling stew, reaches his hand up to grab the rim and leaps inside.

XV

Necrocide

"Right over there! On the other side of that rotting log!" Martha shouts.

"I've never seen a dead body before," Vince marvels. "I wonder what it's like."

"It's like a normal body, except, you know…they don't move around much anymore."

"That's incredibly thoughtful, Martha. Thank you."

Martha and Vince lead the pack, with Jared, Richard, and Adriana following closely behind. They have traveled through the woods, across a river, taken two wrong turns and got entirely lost once, all to be here now. As evidenced by their positions in order, Martha and Vince are excited, Jared and Adriana are apprehensive, and Richard couldn't care less.

"What does it look like?" Adriana hesitates to ask.

"A body! Like a normal man, only dead! Hurry!" Martha shouts, picking up the pace. The five pre-pubescents approach the fallen tree which hides the fallen man.

"Who's going first?" the bashful Jared asks.

"You are, dork." Adriana shoves Jared from behind, as he lurches forward and gathers himself.

"Leave him alone, Adriana. I'm going first, duh," Vince asserts.

"Who voted you the boss?" Martha questions. "It's my dead body, I found him which means I'm going first."

"Exactly, you've already seen him. Move, I'm going first." Vince bumps Martha out of the way and leapfrogs over the top of the massive trunk.

The other four children nervously await an assessment.

"Well?" Adriana asks, bored.

"Whoa..." Vince lets loose from the other side of the log.

Martha leaps on the log to peek, followed by Jared, Richard, and finally Adriana. A middle-aged man is slumped over with his back against the tree, backpack laid beside him.

"See, told you. Doesn't look like anything," Martha pipes up.

"Oh, shut up, Martha. You couldn't WAIT to get here," Vince retorts.

The man stirs, raising his hand to adjust his hat. "Who's there?"

Four of the kids gasp and drop down to the ground cowering away from the stranger. Only Jared is unfazed. "Are you okay, mister?" he asks, swinging his leg over to drop next to the man while his four friends eavesdrop from the other side of the log.

"I'm doing just fine. Was out here on a hike and bumped my noggin, so I stopped to take a nap. I'm feeling better and should be on my way now."

"Let me help you up, at least, sir."

"Oh, alright. If you insist," the man says over the sound of twigs crunching beneath his boot as he digs in to stand. A second of silence precedes a loud crash and a thud against the log, causing Martha, Vince, Richard, and Adriana to leap in fright.

"Guys…" Jared tails off from the other side of the log. "I think he's dead."

Vince hops over first to prove his courage after hiding before. "Holy crap, he IS dead."

"He was already dead," Martha adds as she joins them.

"How could he be dead if he was just talking?" Richard asks, jumping over with Adriana.

"He was alive and now he's dead!" Jared shouts, pale in the face.

"Wait a minute," Adriana asserts, "how could a dead guy even be talking in the first place?"

"He WASN'T dead! Didn't you hear him say he hit his head?"

Martha, Vince, Richard, and Adriana shake their heads no.

"All we could hear was a muffled voice. A MAN'S voice, so we know it wasn't you, Jared. No offense," Vince adds.

Jared stares at them, exasperated.

"So, he woke up when you landed next to him, then suddenly died?" Richard questions.

"Yeah, well…sorta. He started talking to me, but as I was helping him to his feet, he went limp and heavy, then I dropped him against the tree trunk."

"Relax, Jared, it was probably just a delayed reaction from him hitting his head earlier," Martha assesses.

"Yeah, or maybe he hit his head again when you let him go and died then," Adriana says.

Jared sweats anxiously.

"What's that mark on your arm, Jared? Is that where the man grabbed you?" Vince asks.

"Looks painful," Martha comments.

Jared inspects the wound on the top side of his wrist. A darkened handprint, resembling something between a bad bruise and frostbite, is etched into his skin and burnt along the outline. He has never noticed it before, but suddenly it feels incredibly cold and scorching at the same time.

"Gross," Adriana mutters.

"Did he grab you that hard?" Vince asks.

"No, I…I don't think so. He grabbed my hand, not my wrist, and this is a left handprint. He would have grabbed my right hand with his right… right?!"

"You tell us," Martha snarks.

But Richard only stares, eyes wide and aghast. "He has the mark! Everyone back away, now!"

"Don't be an idiot, what mark? It's clearly a handprint," Vince argues.

"Jared carries the cold mark of Death! I read about it in a book one time, just trust me!"

"But…HOW, Richard? That doesn't make any sense," Martha says.

"There are many ways to get the mark, but we absolutely cannot touch him."

"Freak," Adrianna winces, standing closest to Jared.

"Ooh, scary bruise! Careful, everybody! If you touch it, you might turn into a toad!" Vince dashes over facetiously and slaps his left hand down on the mark. The air escapes him. His eyes nearly burst forth from his head as he falls flat on his back and stiff as a board. The four friends stare breathlessly.

"You're stupid. Get up," Martha chastises.

Vince remains petrified, face contorted.

Adriana laughs at his expression, breaking the tension. Martha attempts to scare him by pretending to stomp on his face, while Jared finally allows his shoulders to drop. What a relief, knowing not only did he not kill that poor man, but he didn't harm his best friend, either.

"You really had me going, Richard! Death's cold mark! You butthead," Jared cackles. Martha and Adriana laugh alongside him. "And Vince, quite the performance! I was so nervous, I almost pissed my pants, Richard!"

Richard is unamused.

"Imagine that, such a silly story. Ooga booga!" Jared gestures with his hands as he lunges for Adriana, grabbing both her shoulders. Her body goes rigid and she falls forward, smashing her face on a large rock.

Martha and Richard go catatonic, while Jared remains still and begins to feel rather ill.

"Little boys and girls shouldn't play games alone in the woods." An older woman stands behind them, causing Martha and Richard to surge out of their skin and scatter in opposite directions. Jared quivers, but now feels he deserves whatever fate may come his way. The woman walks up directly to him and smiles.

"Who…who are you?" he stammers.

"What would be most pleasant for you to call me? Mom?" she asks him.

"No, that's kind of weird…my mom died during childbirth. It was my fault."

"Nonsense. Although, I'm aware of the story," the woman says, reaching out to grab Jared's arm.

"No, don't!"

She grasps his forearm and flips it over, placing her left hand over the mark with an exact fit. Jared shoots his eyes up to meet her steely gaze, losing himself in the vacuous caverns of her cold eyes.

"Wait, who are you? The last three people that touched me died."

"Yes, I see that. I am nobody, just a friendly stranger. I bet you haven't had many friends before."

"Certainly not anymore."

The woman scoffs, brandishing half a grin for the first time. She is middle-aged and pretty, yet enigmatic and magnetic. Someone Jared would follow, for better or worse.

"You will find little use for companions, anyway. They will only slow you down."

"Where am I going?" Jared asks.

"Anywhere you wish. The world is yours now."

Jared lowers his head, deep in thought. "Why now? I'm so confused, my friends are dead and I don't even know what to call you."

"You were baptized in the fires of loss, Jared, from the second you burst forth into the world. That's how you got that mark, touched by Death at birth yet still you live. Your friends, acquaintances, classmates, and any family you have left will all, eventually, meet their end by your hand if you let it happen. How does that sound?"

"Awful! It sounds absolutely awful! I've been alone my whole life so far and now you're telling me nothing will ever get better for the rest of it?!"

"I understand you're upset, sweet boy, truly I do. Please know none of this is your fault," the woman pacifies him.

"But…I'm a good person! I can't do evil things! I have already killed three people today alone and you expect me to just accept it?!"

"Nothing has value that which has not been assigned. There is no such thing as good or evil except for your own perception of it. If you view those three deaths as a tragedy, then you are at fault. If their deaths were an inevitability, then you are merely an impartial messenger."

Jared feels a tear slide down his cheek as his shoulders droop under massive weight.

"Everyone dies," she continues. "Every person has an hour glass that activates the second they're born. The only variable is how much sand each person has at their disposal, which is life's greatest mystery. Don't you WISH you could have that information? Memento mori, live each day to the fullest because it may be your last."

"I don't know…that seems like too much responsibility for one person, especially a kid."

"Which is one of many reasons why you're so important! You are the catalyst of joy, he who stops life from being little more than an endless chore. They know you're coming at some point, but the mystery brings excitement. Life wouldn't be fun if it never stopped."

"I guess…wait, ME?!" Jared shouts.

"Yes, you."

"Why?!"

"You faced death today for the first time since receiving your mark. Even though the man you found turned out to be alive, it was his supposed demise to awaken your dormant destiny, which is also how I found you. That handprint is deeper than skin, Jared," the woman says, running her fingers over the mark again. "What other choice do you really have?"

"None, I guess…what do you need from me?"

"Compliance."

"And if I don't? No offense, lady, but what else do I have to lose that you can use against me?"

Her gaze sharpens as a layer of frost cascades through the trees surrounding them. The forest transforms from a traditional brown and green landscape to that of a glacial light blue and white. Sounds of cracking ice circle them as Jared's position is swallowed up by hopeless arctic atmosphere, which should be chilling him to the bone. Vince and Adriana creek behind him, standing over each shoulder and whispering in Jared's ears.

"Endless nightmares, Jared, death everywhere you look. Every plant, animal, and person you speak to shall perish. Cold. You will peer at yourself in the mirror and see only decay." The deeper and softer voices enter each ear and combine within his head to create torrential discomfort. "Comply, Jared, or this will be your eternity. We guarantee it."

Jared is frozen in fear and unable to move. A large hand firmly grasps the back of his neck and jerks him around to face his enemies. It is the nameless man who should be slumped over dead against the log, now standing tall between Jared's fallen friends. Six black eyes shoot harmful intentions within the terrified young boy, whose breathing begins to falter from either crippling fear or bitter cold, possibly both.

The woman, who Jared briefly thought of as an ally, begins to speak from a place of nowhere, encompassing his position from the inside out yet her figure is gone.

"Let go, dear boy, let go now and this will all end. No more suffering for you, if only you allow me in." The three corpses speak her words through decrepit mouths, obsidian eyes staring forward blankly.

"You told me I would already be surrounded by this for the rest of my life! Is this not what death is?" Jared screams at nothing in particular.

"Do you want to see death or BE it? You can either drink from the well as you wish, or you can be pushed into it to drown. Comply."

"Won't I get used to this suffering after enough time?"

"The pestilence of a foolish young boy," her voice booms, knocking frost from the dying leaves.

Footsteps resound in the forest, shaking the ground underneath Jared's feet. Shadows emerge from the trees in all directions and form a tight perimeter around Jared, Vince, Adriana, and the nameless man. Everyone Jared has ever known slowly steps closer; his school teachers, classmates, friends, and family, all deceased and pushing forward. They begin to whisper the horrors of how they met their ends in a dissonant storm of voices while trudging closer. Jared's mother walks closest and stares down at him, shaking her head in disappointment. He drops to his knees, trembling.

"Make it go away, all of it! I give in!"

"No, I don't believe you have."

The crowd of cadavers parts to reveal Richard and Martha as Jared's fourth grade teacher pushes them both forward.

"Touch their faces," the woman commands.

"None of this is real, so they won't get hurt, right?"

"Touch their faces to prove your loyalty."

Jared's hands quiver at his sides as the surrounding voices grow unbearably loud. The pain of a thousand screams rings within his head until he feels like he might explode. His arms shoot up to grab the throats of Martha and Richard, who instantly crumble to the ground at his feet.

Jared forces his eyes shut to avoid staring at the hordes of encroaching dead, and opens them again to see everyone gone and the arctic frost returned to green leaves. The two friends, who had nearly escaped the forest before being yanked back, lay still at his feet while the rest of the surrounding area seems unaware of the previous event.

The woman approaches Jared from behind and rests her hands on his tight shoulders. "Please don't test me again, Jared. Life can ALWAYS get worse and it is never wise to call that bluff. OR, you might find yourself quite comfortable beside me. Look at them."

Jared feels the ground dissolve beneath him as the woman forces him within inches of Martha's face.

"Look," she continues. "Look into their faces and get comfortable with what you've done. This is all I need from you, then you will be free."

The comparatively lush forest jolts back into the arctic tundra of enveloping dead. The woman's face devolves into a devilish pit of bottomless blackness, pushing forward toward Jared. "If you are unable to follow through on your duties, THIS will be your eternity. Do you understand?" The suddenly deep vibrato chills him to the bone, a sensation he has never felt until now.

"NO! Take it away, make it stop!" Clammy hands grasp at his arms and legs, pulling him downward beneath the surface. The woman smiles and it all disappears once again.

"Good. Very good, Jared. We all have choices, but sometimes that choice is more of an imposed illusion than our actual free will."

The boy weeps, both for himself and also thinking of the pain he will inflict upon others to be free from this living nightmare.

"You do not trust me yet, although you will learn to. You're not a bad person, sweet child, nor am I, believe it or not. You will be asked to give passage to both saints and sinners, some you feel good about taking, and others that will haunt your mind for eons to come. That is not your choice. I suggest you get used to following directions without emotional attachment. Your first task is near," the woman warns him.

"How will I know what to do?"

"You will know." She grabs his hand and turns it over. "The pain in your arm will be unbearable at first until you learn to heed the internal whispers. That is to ensure you don't fail. I must go now, you're on your own."

"Wait! What if I need help?" Jared clamors.

"Look around you, I am everywhere."

"That's it? Now I just have to do this for the rest of my life?"

"Sweet boy, what makes you so sure you're alive?" The woman bends down to kiss Jared's forehead and turns to walk away, fading between the trees. Within a matter of minutes, a hiking couple marches through the clearing. Jared drops to his knees in agony.

"Hello, there! Can you please help us? We appear to be walking in circles and daylight is wearing thin! Oh, my goodness, help the boy up, he's hurt!"

"You hold him still, I'll give him CPR!"

XVI

As Within So Without

White walls in a rectangular shaped windowless dead-end. Repetitious anesthesia propagated from perennial lockdown. Tedium. Atrocious bed, putrid food, a lonesome home in which to reside. Padded walls all around, but for safety or security, and security for whom? Pencil rhythmically scratching twenty-four weight white journal paper, as good as a music box in deafening silence.

Today is Tuesday, or Thursday, definitely one of the T days. Although, given enough consideration, it could also be Sunday, two days removed from my favorite day, Tuesday, or possibly two days further so it's Thursday. Too many twos to go through today. Today is either Sunday, Twosday, or Thursday, yet it could also be the eighth day of the week with us never the wiser. Of one thing I am certain, it has been one thousand seven hundred thirty-three days, six hours and…twenty-one minutes of confinement. Without a doubt.

One day life could be special, if I let it. The only obstacle in my way is me, per usual, though who else would be a worthy opponent? Dark shadows and gloomy visions block my tomorrow, so be it, but I will prevail. One half of me, either the light or the dark half, perhaps split into two quarters of each, shall succeed and I will immediately join the team of the victor. What other choice do I have? The loser will be dead.

This is my reality. It may be different from yours, and very likely is, but don't let that distract you from the truth. Nothing is as it seems and I am but a spectator, as are you and your friends and their friends, and so on. We are all watching our biopic films play out in real-time. I think mine is a horror movie.

The space I occupy, or rather rent, is shared with others, though we don't confer much. Each of us spends an inordinate amount of time plotting an escape, for beyond these walls lies greener pastures and salvation, I'm sure of it, though this truth cannot be easily proven, maybe not at all. Should we escape, by virtue of nostalgia, the prison cell may then be viewed as the greener grass. Each of us stands in a corner, facing it with intentions of liberation, backs toward each other to ensure we all think alone as fractured entities of a supposed greater being. We could have been free months ago had we worked together, take my word for it. It is tough being the only enlightened one.

Every now and then, one of the others will drown the rest of us out, hammering at their corner with reckless abandon. Us other three, now lesser persons in the shadow of whomever so happens to be of prominence, cower under the weight of their dominance. It won't last long, nothing ever does, but as of now, the only recourse is to wait for this over-achiever to tire out and allow another to take a turn. I feel as though I have not had a go in quite some time now, and the anticipation is causing me to grow uncharacteristically restless.

They and I, the four of us in this room, have shockingly little in common aside from the communal cell we share. They make for dreadful company and I certainly wish I could be alone, which may explain why I subconsciously allow them to chip away at their corners instead of taking extra time for my own. More than anything, they wish to be free, while I only yearn for solitude in whatever manner that occurs.

Six months have passed since we began this endeavor to escape. My corner is the deepest sunk, most ironically, as I have spent the least amount of time on it, yet have worked the hardest. Softer material, maybe. I spend more of my effort dreaming about what lies beyond this wall, and then beyond the next set of boundaries after that. My excavated corner provides a decent cave to hide within if I face the wall to drown out the room. Oh, the thoughts they think, I can hear them!

Our cell has been outfitted with four more fresh prisoners, each stationed between two corners. They wasted no time in trying to catch up to our efforts, transforming the living area from an oblong square to a dilapidated octagon. Somehow, these new inmates have been even worse than the first and I have chosen not to speak with them. Pity, if only we could all think alike, if only…yet which of us eight would be the RIGHT one?

Inside my cave, I can hear the echoes of a life left behind, whisperings from a bygone era. The free life, the world outside, beckons me yet I can't place the origin. Three errant complainers have now turned to seven and I can't drown out their thoughts for very long at all! I wish they would just sit still so I could think my way through, although my thoughts present a problem of their own. Befuddling and raucous. A river flowing rampantly yet my best attempts equate to a small rock sitting helplessly in the center.

Three days have passed since I found the time to mine my corner wall. The others must be catching up to my progress judging by how quiet they have been. Mental health is important, thus I allowed myself a break for rest, mostly taking time to meditate and gaze out my imaginary cave window in quiet contemplation. A dream can only begin with a thought, which may then become reality. I must make a reminder that once I am out of here, I should quote myself on that. Brilliant.

I spoke too soon. What had been busy silence has become uproarious cacophony between the seven entities, and for the life of me I cannot find a place to drown it out. One person wishes for strength, another for time, while the third asks for patience. Perhaps if I wasn't the only one wishing for seclusion, this would be an easier task to see through.

Their pleas have made it impossible to do much of anything at all, let alone that which I should be doing. Envy, sorrow, and rage flood my mind, while the final whisper asks for nothing. Perfect contentment, the world that one lives in. The other six would all be furious if they knew.

The day eventually came when their voices grew larger than my defenses could bear, and unfortunately the influence of such notions began to invade my every thought. I sat within my cave, digging diligently if not entirely enthusiastically, and I grew envious over my neighbors' positions in relation to my own. Who cares if they were ahead, behind, or otherwise, they must be doing better than me, I was certain of it and thus my progress ground to a halt.

Slamming my tools against the adjacent wall in a rage, I stuck my head out of the crevice to take stock of the others' progression. Looking right first, I discover my nearest cellmate to be staring at me already. Peering to my left, that neighbor shows only the back of their head as they stare to their left at their neighbor, who is also looking left at another facing the same direction, continuing several people in a circle until the person two over from my right is glaring at the back of my neighbor.

While I wasted my attention focusing on these seven others, they were all watching me in return! I could have gotten far ahead of the competition, but instead, my focus was thrown into a bottomless pit of worry as they were distracted by the noise of progress. Speaking of which, I do not even recall how far I got, if at all. For shame. I could have accomplished so much, had they not distracted me!

In the thralls of going through it, the doldrums, I slump into the corner for several days and hope for a better mood to take hold before carrying onward. I had been in such a rush, so aggressively pursuing the finish line, that I forgot to breathe for a minute, if not JUST a moment, which consequently turned from one to thousands in an instant. No matter.

Competition got the better of me and obscured my better judgement, but no more! Deep breaths and clarity for me from now on, nothing less ever again. This cave I have dug for myself, my shadow home, has grown to be ever more comfortable the longer I spend in it. The less I wish to be out of it, the greater it becomes. My strength has also returned and I feel as though I could smash through the remaining stone in one final blow, if only I wanted to. Yeah, if only.

Three more glorious days pass in the blink of an eye when an itch begins to come over me. It is negligible at first, though present, yet growing rapidly with each descending thought. Just ignore it, my own worst advice yet, for it claws at me worse each time I breathe in harder to will it away. The scratching noise burrows its way through my admittedly weak defenses, which had been at ease for several days preceding this and enjoying the break. Now, though, as my tranquil mood tumbles into territories unknown in the blackened depths of naught, this sound is all I can hear. Nothing else, only nails on a chalkboard through my days and nights.

Eventually, on day four of pacing, the abrasive nuisance grows loud enough for me to hear it clearly beyond the static. Their voices, all seven of them, return in a monsoonish wind storm. Strength, envy, patience, sorrow, and rage swarm my system in an electrical surge, every impulse consumed by their alternating waves. What is it I want? Currently, for the voices to cease existing.

My confidence peaks as I feel equipped to fight them off, then jealous of my neighbors for not being crushed under the weight of the same rock. I calm myself for long enough to reassess, only to then feel bitter sadness, as if the cycle will never end and I will be stuck with these voices forever. Frustration looms, sending me into a frenzy at my lack of control riding the parabola of emotions with no brakes. Time passes slowly, but eventually crescendos into a blaze. The inferno washes over me and nothing makes sense aside from the ringing in my ears. Hatred…rage. I can't think clearly over this blinding caustic anger and the desire to be free from this cage even if it would mean bashing my own head through the remaining concrete. Either the wall will split or I will, as long as I'm liberated.

Just as I felt I could feel no more, at the edge of sanity where clarity kisses berserk, the anger evaporates into a black hole within. Nothing. For a brief period of time between fury and the rebound of strength, I felt zero. No thought, nor emotion, only peace. Quiet contentment and happy to be taking space in this moment of existence. THIS is what I want, MY desire in the rare lapse of external influence. I would do anything to seize the moment, if only I could bottle this emotion, or lack thereof and bring new meaning to peace and quiet whenever I wish.

The sensation of excitement over feeling a lack of anything stimulates the senses enough to spark a bit of enthusiasm, kicking my motivation back into overdrive and I feel strong enough to break through these walls again. So begins the cycle once more. It's THEM out there, their errant emotions seeping into my routine. I cannot stand such a lack of control! Or maybe I will be able to soon, whenever they allow me to. The voices are too sharp, too overwhelming, I wish to return to nothingness.

And before I know it, I do. Blissful existence. Never wanting anything more than to breathe in the air of this cave because that is what is available in the space where I am present. Lovely latency, tranquil times. Level-head and clear thoughts, comforts which I am not accustomed to. The equivalency of a storm colliding with a sunny day, riding the high while feeling nothing at all. But the sensation rising within, whichever one it may be, is unwelcome. I do not want it, I reject this feeling.

The arc of perception running the gamut once again, yet this time they bleed together like emotions blending into brand new colors. The feelings of despair, longing, and sheer horror rival the cavalcade of strength through sorrow, yet they all begin to pour through my fingers like rapidly melting ice. Those emotions I had known before to be familiar yet vexing are now hanging from the end of an oily and frayed rope, slipping through my fingers faster than I can reconcile. Regret pours into nostalgia. These new feelings are worrisome, will I be able to handle them? Or will they overtake me like an impending wave?

Pull the strings tighter, hold on with everything you've got. Through my focus on old friends, so to speak, one particular phase burrows its way through. Trickling inward, unidentifiable by instinct, but immediately familiar nonetheless. Rage, my old friend, yes…unfiltered, venomous rage forcing its way throughout my system like water bursting through a broken dam. I quickly lay down my guard, no reason to argue, for this is an unwinnable battle as I have found in each skirmish before. I was defeated the instant manifestation began.

I exit my cave with renegade intentions and stomp toward my left-most neighbor, who is still not facing my direction. I bare my teeth and slaughter him with ease, something he never saw coming, though he is no doubt surprised nevertheless as my pickaxe is driven through his skull. I leave the disfigured entity in a crippled heap on the floor, no more recognizable to me than a pile of dust or discarded waste. Good riddance, nuisance and destroyer of concentration. Be gone with you but not nearly soon enough.

One voice from my head is silenced, yet it only amplifies the other six in return. Loudest in the back, that being the most merciless of the bunch, carrying over the top of the others who cower before it. The wolf in the henhouse, or perhaps more suitably, sinners standing before their angered god. None of them ever stood a chance.

I do not believe I can take any more, none at all if even only a moment longer would rid me of all my ails. What is there for one to do? Nothing brings relief, nothing except giving in to the voices, although only one rings true while the others shout over each other in a panic. That cadence in the back, though, I understand you perfectly fine, if not too well. My enclosed world looked a bit brighter when I rid it of just one screaming tone, might not two feel better? Maybe four, or even six? I no longer have the inner strength to resist, the urge toward fortitude has dissipated like a departing echo. The next neighbor over must be annihilated so that I may be free. There is no other way.

His head is turned, staring at the back of his neighbor's head next to him. For as much as I wish to harm this person, I also feel a sense of longing, if not jealousy entirely. How can he be so calm while I burn inside? His attention is occupied by only one thing, while war wages inside my head. It is unequivocally unfair.

Off with his head as he is savagely dismembered in the same fashion as our mutual neighbor before, leading me to feel instantly better but also much more vengeful. A notable amount of pressure is relieved within and the storm opens up to reveal a single ray of light, however far away as it may be. The fallen fellow prisoner lays on the grimy floor in chunks adorned with various pickaxe holes scattered throughout the scraps. I pick up the largest piece of head only to drop it with these twitching hands, watching it descend rapidly until it shatters like glass on the ground. It IS glass, the entire body jaggedly fractured, which is inconsequential to the benefit of one less voice vexing me.

What a shame, this pile at my feet, so eager to escape our lockup in the same way I was, but fell short. I'm sorry for being better, truly, for if you had been able, you would be standing over my fragments rather than it being this way. I wanted it more. I kick the debris away and circle onward. They all have to die so their voices will go with them, their thoughts and wishes too. Each quieted voice opens the door for the others to grow in their stead.

The pickaxe goes to work of its own will, shredding clockwise through the following three cellmates like I was born to be here and thrilled to do it. Three remain, myself included, while the distractions have subsided beneath a whisper, yet still more than nothing if only slightly. One tells me to wait it out, take my time and visualize a better plan of attack. It implores to lean into logic over emotion and wait for circumstances to evolve naturally as they were meant.

The second voice domineers the other and demands action from us both. It insists we are complacent, nihilistic even, and should claw our way out in any manner necessary, unconditionally and without compromise. The contrast has forced a stalemate. Stop and go, fight or flight, whenever one voice gains ground the other comes through the rear and takes the lead. Which is right, or rather, which is less incorrect? Dark and light, submit to the impulse or resist the urge?

Both remaining occupants now stand facing me in the center of the room, the one to my left with his left hand outstretched, and he to the right holding out his right. Electrical frequency of emotional shifting leaves my feet feeling like cement blocks sinking to the bottom of a lake, and besides, I wouldn't know which side to choose even if I were able to move freely. Cold depths overtake me, yet it is only the implied visual drawing confusion from a manufactured thought process- needless to say my mental welfare is in peril at best.

How does one choose a side when both are promising great things? I can remain in stasis for only so long, as it has been proven change follows action, not thoughts. Hot and cold intentions mix within to brew a twister of a mindset. It was easier when there were seven voices bickering instead of just these two. One synapse links to another, and another, to form a chain of action that twitches my muscles into motion beginning in the fingers.

I grasp the pick-axe tightly and swing it wildly through the ear of the left member, yanking it out with force and rotating another full turn into the right cell-mate's forehead. Their bodies dropping to the floor is not enough, entirely and not nearly enough, thus I continue to hack into each of them fairly until they return to dust like all the rest.

The voices that have plagued my mind for the better part of what feels like the past half-century have finally and at long last begun to descend down the well of obscurity. There is no more speaking, no more wishes, complaints, or aspirations to endure, no more disturbing thoughts planted in my head from someone else's desires. Only nothing, sweet silence surrounding my ears inside and out, greets me now and the want of naught returns.

The last person who felt perfect contentment was me the whole time, the real me, clouded by seven others hellbent on ensuring I would not feel normal for as long as they could not. I lay in the center of the coated floor and feel it drop from beneath, floating along the surface of a river, although my body and the ceiling lay still. This is what satisfaction feels like, wants and needs dissolved inside the human form, of which plenty lay scattered around me. Gratification, the sensation of enjoyment in the present, considering what happened in the past for me to have reached this state now, and what is coming to me in the future because of it. Having reached peak enjoyment on this smooth concrete, it eventually comes time to rise and continue loving every breath taken and each second passed without distraction or interference. I never wanted anything more than nothing, and after great delay it is finally mine with permanence.

A brief whisper enters my ear that it may be wise to clean up the victim debris before it causes issue in my blank sanctum. It's not that I WANT to, and certainly not that I NEED to, yet their body parts crowding the room obscures the essence of what constitutes 'nothing' and I can't have that. Returning to my manufactured cave, I grab a shovel with intentions to scoop the piles of trash into a corner.

The first downed inmate, that to my left, lays in a heap with only the head remaining on top, face down in soot. Perhaps the heads should be stored in a separate location from their deconstructed vessels beneath, which could only be mixed together. The heads, though, should be lined up to honor those whose sacrifice ensured my sanity.

I grab the fleshy skull and lift it to my face so I may see it more clearly in such dim light. By all that is good and holy, and I have not inspected myself in a mirror in quite some time, but the face is mine! Every detail as I remember, including the long hair which I have not bothered to trim in over a year. My hands tremble, the opposite of nothing, as trepidation makes a brief appearance to remind me of my mortality. Life is full of fear, even in here, and this is the perfect reminder to appreciate any time I am privileged enough to not feel.

This is surely the occurrence of temporary psychosis, a fever dream following the adrenaline rush of finally silencing all doubt. I have been under extreme duress for far too long it seems, symptoms of an overly-taxed system, I'm sure. Forget it. I walk to the next stack of bodily pieces and brush the head off first so I don't compromise my vision with what I think I just saw. Carefully sweeping the pile into the same corner, I take a deep breath and walk back toward the second head.

Lifting it to my eyes, my arms instinctively throw it toward the center of the room with a twitch. Another face identical to my own, yet I can't be sure without viewing it again. Why waste the time? Keep moving forward, always, although maybe I will brush the dust and save the heads for last to enhance my efficiency.

Sweeping the rest of the five piles into the designated corner, and tossing the heads into the center with my eyes closed so as not to influence my own position, I finally complete the task and can return to doing nothing as designed. Who cares about those heads and how they hypothetically look? Not me! Not me...

Fine, just one look for reassurance, then I will ruminate no more, a promise to myself even I am not sure I can keep. With my hand raised to my eyes and walking to the center of the room, I take a peak and begin to feel rather ill almost instantaneously. All seven heads, all facing me now, all share my identical features without fail. They stare, blankly and dumbly, like statuesque beings I never intended to create. The only difference between them would be their expressions, as one appears determined, while another looks concerned.

I fall to my back side in shock, both hands covering my mouth for fear of a shriek escaping in this vacuum. Seven faces adorning seven heads of my own facial fortitude, how can this be?! The nothingness I so longed for now feels like crushing emptiness under this revelation. Everything I asked for, over the course of years upon years, finally comes to fruition at my own hand and now I can't handle the pressure?

Oh, what a difference mental outlook makes in perception! In this room, what only just previously felt like vindicating freedom between these walls has morphed into a tomb bereft of the strength to continue the mission of escape through my dug-out cave. I will die here on this decrepit floor, the eighth face joining the fallen seven, the matter of my body melding into the others in a pile of fine powder. My brethren, apparently, my fallen selves.

XVII

Fear of Life

OCTOBER 1ST,

It pains me to admit as a veteran author, but my writing has taken a horribly unproductive turn over the last several months. Between life stresses, personal relationships straining, various health issues, distractions, and general complacency, it has felt nearly impossible to sit down and pay this project the attention it deserves. I have reserved time alone in a cabin on the mountainside, deeply secluded, to finish my novel in the proper state of mind with no outside interference for the first time in months. Having just arrived earlier this evening, I feel that perhaps I should settle in for the night before committing myself to any serious work, even though I am in tune with the transition already. After all, the mind is a serious muscle and must be properly tended to or the consequences may be dire, particularly for those who earn a living off that muscle.

Inside this leather journal, an old family heirloom that has gone unused until now, I will document my time here as a form of writing exercise between working on the novel. Practice, if you will, and practice is everything. I should turn in for the night, as there will be plenty of time to write in my near future.

OCTOBER 2ND,

The area surrounding my cabin is appropriately quiet, while the atmosphere inside the home is perfectly conducive to writing, although something just feels…OFF? I have been unable to focus throughout the morning and afternoon, which led me to use the time instead to unpack my belongings and prepare for what lies ahead instead of immediately diving into writing. There is no rushing the process, as is learned by most writers at some point or another in their careers, presumably early on if they are to have much of a career at all. The entire day has felt like someone was watching me from behind, thus every task has been accompanied by my staring in various directions multiple times like a madman. This feeling is tough to describe due to the apparently fictional nature of the phenomenon, but regardless of how I feel about it, the thought is difficult to ignore. Now it is evening and my novel is no better off for it, as each keystroke sets off a fire alarm of an echo through the empty house and forcing me to jump with a fright at my own actions, darting my eyes frantically around the room to spot this would-be intruder. I suppose my imagination has gotten the best of me, being alone in a strange new environment and coming from a bustling city to this rural hideaway. I expected the adjustment to take time and effort, undoubtedly, though this is a bit rich.

As of this entry, I have yet to make any actual progress with my intended writing project, instead jotting down journal logs about my failed attempts to work, yet such is the process of creation. Sometimes feast, sometimes famine. I go through periods lush with ideas, blazing through pages of excellent work at a manic pace, followed by phases where I sit and toil, such as today. Not to worry, the struggle will benefit the overall project. I came here to write an amazing novel, not to write an easy one.

That being said, I hope to relax rather quickly and be free from this eerie weight on my shoulders. I suppose neurotic behavior wouldn't be entirely out of character, although that is different from FEELING like something is out of whack rather than thinking it. Perhaps it would be best to sit outside on the porch and take in the atmosphere with a glass of whiskey or three, have a bit of play and put off work until tomorrow.

OCTOBER 3RD,

Still not relaxed as hoped, still feel watched. Started writing early this morning, but the exposure is getting to me. The cabin, while providing the ideal backdrop for an isolated writing retreat, also gives off the impression of being a sitting duck while enemies wait to pounce from all sides. The back wall of the house, featuring a typical sliding glass door, is also surrounded by massive windows stretching six-feet wide on either side of the slider and twenty-feet up to the roof. Sitting inside the cabin at night with the lack of civilization out there feels like life ends at those glass panels and all sorts of dark entities are peering back without me knowing it. I stare outside and see nothing, returning to my work, losing confidence and looking around again in a panic within a minute. Repeat the process. I have been known to be a control freak in the past, but the thought of sitting here vulnerable and rendered virtually naked while who-knows-what watches my every move is rather hard to stomach. Because of this, I have moved my base of operations to the basement, no pun intended, where there are no windows.

Rationally speaking, drowning myself deeper in writing the actual novel would solve most of my current issues, or just the one issue, actually, which is easier said than done. Burrowing paranoia reaming out my psyche was an unintended side effect of trying to write this book, and it arose at the most inopportune time imaginable. The pitfalls of being a horror author coming home to roost, my imaginative demons run amuck.

OCTOBER 4TH,

I am utterly convinced someone is trying to kill me. There is a figure, I am see-ing it everywhere, out every window, in the shadows of every room upstairs while I am up there. Each time I allow myself to be vulnerable, it knows, and that's when it attempts a move on me. Little is this malevolent agent aware, I am an author and my imagination is stronger than any plot it may conjure. I will not get got by he or she of inferior intellect, I shall not be bested in games of the mind. I will not let my guard down again.

I have stored plenty of food in the basement, for it would be unwise to leave once night has fallen. The process has been the same each time I have ventured out of this room; shut and lock the door behind me so nothing can follow, then inspect every nook and cranny of the basement before settling in to write. Once it has been deemed safe and free of invaders, I barricade the door with a set of wood shelves, which would serve as a loud alarm should anyone actually make it through. Admittedly, in that case, I am not sure what I would do.

Here I find myself now, burning the midnight oil in my self-imposed dungeon, while the upper floor of my cabin could have anything happening at any given time. Predators, demonic spirits, or otherwise unwelcome guests may be throwing themselves a party on the upper floors at my expense. No matter, I will hide down here in the safety of darkness and this bottle of bour-bon, both of which help me cope with the threat, and the task, at hand. If this book does not get done in a reasonable amount of time, and to a reasonable level of quality, I will then surely be in more trouble than simply having a murderer on my trail.

OCTOBER 5TH,

Writer's block. The inside of my brain feels physically abused by the level of effort expended in my bout for survival, and the creative side suffers for it.

Word retrieval is non-existent, nor could I think of a good idea to save my life even if it would help stop the monster after me.

Nothing has improved with this situation. I imagine, even if I were to leave the cabin and flee home, I would be followed and inevitably murdered when the killer no longer finds amusement in my misery. The best I can do now is stay out of sight, dwell in my basement cave, and complete the mission that led me here in the first place. The book needs to be finished above all else.

As I write this, I hear footsteps overhead on the wood floorboards. This person is no longer hiding it, he or she is now simply waiting for me to come out, yet I remain one step ahead. Fortunately for me, I have a bathroom down here, as well as every bit of food in the house and plenty of single malt. If all else fails, maybe it will grow bored and bring mischief to the next house in line, wherever that is. Every so often, the doorknob jiggles, knowing full well the door is locked, but just reminding me how hopelessly trapped I am. My thoughts are consumed and the only subject matter I have been able to write is about this experience. As a fiction writer, maybe this makes sense to do?

OCTOBER 6TH,

My mental state is in decline. I have absolutely no recourse. The face I see in every dark crevice of the cabin has taken residence inside my eyelids when I try to finally rest. The severity of this obsession cannot be healthy, nor would I imagine it to be incredibly productive, either.

Something else has come to my attention, something I can't definitively prove, of course…but it seems my assailant has access to my mind. It sounds insane, even more so now that it has been officially recorded, yet I KNOW what I know, and this monster is ahead of me every step of the way. Each thought I have gets intercepted from brain to paper and acted out for its amusement and my anguish.

Whatever I fear, it exploits. Wherever I stare, it appears. If I look toward the door at the top of the stairs, within a couple seconds there will be a knock. If I pick a location to stare at on my ceiling, any spot at all, the monster will tap its foot on the floor above, once, twice, three times like clockwork, every time.

This is a nightmare, only I am very much awake, unfortunately. It pains me to say for fear of it coming true, although I have already thought it so it is too late anyway…I don't believe I will be walking out of here alive. Will I starve to death before the killer finally makes a move? Or do I try to run through the woods like escaping prey? What is the use of worrying either way? I was bested before I ever even arrived here. This person, this…creature has planned for every possible outcome and I am horribly outmatched. Well played.

OCTOBER 7TH,

Fear has taken root so deeply, I cannot control the shakes. My muscles ache, my stomach is full of rocks. The dizziness could either be from utter terror, or my eyes frantically darting around the room to catch the attacker in the act. I don't remember when or how this happened, but my left arm has four deep gashes running diagonally below the wrist. During my sleep, possibly, although I didn't wake. Was I drugged? More psychological warfare for toiling.

WHO is this beast? I thought it human before, but my focus has shifted to a demon attack. This journal may soon turn into a firsthand account of an exorcism, if only I can remember the details. At the very least, this horrific experience will result in world-class material, a lesson taught to me by countless mentors before; everywhere you look, there is something to see, especially with a writer's mind. The silver lining in the sacrifice.

Hours pass between notations. The scratching of pen to paper in the journal is deafening. Each keystroke on the novel seems to act as a rally cry, for every time I get on a roll typing, SOMETHING goes wrong immediately thereafter. Excessive knocking, breathing down my neck. This entity does not wish for me to recount our game of cat-and-mouse because it thrives on secrecy, I know it. Sharing this information with others would expose its strengths, and furthermore, weaknesses. Methods of attack, mostly through the shadows, picking away at my mental fortitude like dripping water dissolving stone. Though, truth be told, that stone feels a lot more like sand the previous few days.

Night has fallen. Darkness begets silence begets dread. I wish I could do anything else at this time, but I must deliberately write lightly enough so as not to arouse suspicion of activity. Lights off outside means no light in my basement cave, both comforting and anguishing. The attacker could be standing right behind me, to my side, or smiling a sinister smile from behind my work. Mocking me. My obsessive habits of checking every corner are also useless. I could bump into the monster any time I move, even walking into the restroom is perilous. The shining light of hope in this blackness is that I won't see my death coming.

I wish you well, I think to myself, but I don't actually believe it. My fate is sealed regardless of my hopes. I wish for you peace and comfort, but I don't anticipate that happening, not in my current state. I wish for closure, that which may come sooner than later, I'm afraid. At least I will know. Sleep...I wish for restful and restorative slumber, but my body is pumping with enough adrenaline to keep me awake for several more weeks, potentially throughout my stay here. Thus, I wait...wait...pray for morning light.

OCTOBER 8TH,

I found him. I'VE FOUND HIM. After ruthlessly struggling for days and nights and weeks on end, or week? I have found the rotten bastard hiding within my wall-mounted mirror, which I believe to be a trick mirror, in truth a window into a hidden room. He, it is a he after all, at least externally, has my face, also part of the illusion to confuse my better sensibilities. We shared a stare down, although he fled once I took a swing at him. Now his deception lies on the floor and staring up at me with thirty faces. Even more exposed.

This is it, the war ends today. I yanked the heavy lamp from my bed's end table and crushed every piece on the floor baring his face, then shattered those remnants thoroughly once more until they reached a fine dust. No more faces, no more insight. Good mourning to me. A subconsciously revealing slip.

Breakfast time rolls around and I nibble on scraps with a mouth drier than the Atacama. Afraid, but otherwise prepared for any outcome after a lengthy imprisonment within these walls. All is quiet until I am struck with my writing chair and knocked to the ground, unconscious for a moment's time. He stands his foot across my throat while I cling to life with my eyes shut. It feels as though his foot resting on the ground is lifted to balance his full weight upon my neck to snuff me out.

My eyes jolt open. No one is there. Breath comes labored and pained, but I have escaped once again, for now. I wonder if it will hurt? Not physically, my physical being already hurts from the attack, but on a deeper level…will it hurt? Beside the fact, I have been hurt many times before but this will be the first and only time feeling the specific sensation. Oh, I hope it feels like nothing. I have been through enough.

As I write this, finishing my telling of the story that has happened to me here, footsteps approach from behind. A hand sets down on my right shoulder to remind me of my limited life left, but otherwise seems to be allowing me to complete relaying the sentiment. This is it, my time has come. Whosoever finds this journal shall know my tale and how I met my end at the hands of a murderer, a shadow creature unseen but deadly as any. My every fear come true, every thought manifested right up until the end. My written word, autobiographical as this demon followed it down to every detail. I could nearly be persuaded into thinking I caused my own demise after a lifetime of creating morbid stories from the pits of my own mind. He is tapping his fingers now, urging me to hurry and accept what lies ahead, whatever that may be, which I will be unable to scribe. It is my time. Godspeed.

"What do you think, do you like it?"

A teenage boy and girl peer around the room inquisitively.

"Yes, I like it. I want this room," the girl announces first.

"You really want to stay in the basement?" their mother asks.

"Anything to give me some alone time from HIM," she sneers at her brother. "It was a long enough car ride already. This will be nice."

"Whatever you wish," her dad mutters, grabbing his son by the shoulder and leading him back upstairs.

"Are you sure this is what you want? Might be awfully lonely down here," the mother speaks at last.

"I do. The privacy is just what I need so I can keep working on my stories."

"I know, and I'm happy to see you pursuing your dreams. That's one of the reasons we chose this place, you know. Several famous authors have stayed in this cabin before," the mom grins. "You know where we'll be, let us know if you need anything." She turns and walks back upstairs.

The teenage girl wanders around the basement with satisfaction, enjoying the prospects of her new home for the next week. On the center of the bed lays a leather-bound book, worn and aged, but immediately drawing her in as a budding writer herself. It looks like a journal. She slowly drags her index and middle fingers over the cover inquisitively and flips it open.

"It pains me to admit as a veteran author, but my writing has taken a horribly unproductive turn over the last several months," she reads aloud from the first page.

XVIII

Eye for an Eye

"Sisters, commence!"

Their bustling slows as a thin breeze whistles through branches dropping dead leaves on their location. A fire blazes mightily at the center of the clearing.

"Do any of you wish to share this evening?"

One hand raises quickly before the others have a chance.

"Sister Margaret. Please." Priestess Elizabeth backs away from the wooden podium, moving so smoothly to appear as floating.

"Sisters, tonight I come forward to ask of thee-"

"Margaret, it is not the 1600s anymore. We must adapt with the common folk, it is an entirely new century."

"Tis, I mean yes, it is. Ahem. Sisters, it hath, I mean have-"

"Has. It HAS," the priestess corrects.

"Thank you. It HAS come to my attention that many of…you…have not been cleaning out your cauldrons properly! The stench of moldy toad gizzards and pickled devil's dung has taken permanent residence inside my nostrils! So, just try to do better, everyone."

Several people stir, some clear their throats. The biting wind rings especially loud among the silence where nothing but crickets speak.

"Thank you, Sister Margaret. How…insightful. Anyone else? Good." Priestess Elizabeth skips over a few raised hands and opens the massive leather-bound book in front of her, removing a quill from her robe and placing it beside the pages. "Shall we officially begin?"

She beckons with a finger for three sisters to enter the clearing, hauling a long log resting on their shoulders. Three bustling burlap sacks hang between them. Chitters of excitement roll through the scores of onlookers.

"Do you smell their purity, sisters? Clean of body and soul for our pleasure alone!"

Sinister sounds of delight follow the announcement. Someone in the middle of the pack raises her hand.

"Yes, Sister?"

"Mary," she responds as she stands. "I'm new here, are those children?"

"More or less. They are young enough to satisfy our needs. Moving on-"

"We're not going to eat them, are we?"

The priestess exhales sharply and massages her twitching eye. "No, Sister Mary, we aren't going to EAT them. That would be repugnant! We are going to grind them into a pulp under stone and use the extract for other purposes."

Sister Mary sits at last as others cheer. Priestess Margaret motions for the three burlap sacks to be hung over the fire, kicking and stirring restlessly from the growing heat beneath.

"In only a few short moments, they will all be dead! Die! Die like the cattle you are! Die for our needs!" the priestess cackles as the woods erupt. A scream escapes one of the sacks but the sound is inaudible over such raucous cheering.

"Ah, yes! I can FEEL your excitement tonight, and why not? It has been quite some time since we have bagged such a haul!" she continues, reaching into her robe and pulling out a small glass jar. "The means to an end, right here in my hand, and what these three will amount to once they are boiled over an open flame."

"We want some, Priestess!" an unknown voice bellows.

"Share with us!" another follows.

"As I will, soon as they are cooked! In the meantime, this portion is reserved for me-" Priestess Elizabeth stops mid-sentence on a dime with the jar raised to her lips, as a flaming arrow shoots through the blackened sky, through the glass, and into her throat. The liquid potion inside the jar ignites and engulfs her upper half in frolicking flames as she gags on the projectile piercing the back of her throat.

Silence and gasps of horror roll through their midst as every member watches their Priestess and leader choke to death and writhe in pain before them. Elizabeth had always been one for pageantry, but is this another instance? A dramatic prank for show or is she truly dead?

Their questions are quickly answered with three more echoing snaps ringing through the valley. Sisters Agnes, Wanda, and Sarah, low priestesses serving under Elizabeth, drop to their knees and desperately grasp at open air for a breath which does not come. Three arrows, one for each, burst through the backs of their heads and stick out their open mouths now.

Chaos and bedlam erupt as each remaining attending sister panics and dives to the floor while their leaders fall like forsaken fruit flies. They all seek makeshift shelter under their seats, tables, and whatever else happens to be in the vicinity. Some dive under fallen tree trunks, while others hide inside rotted wood to bunker during the unforeseen assault.

A hooded figure stands dark and cloaked in the clearing, another flaming arrow ready for their disposal. Every offender disappeared, as they do, and none the easier to dispatch in this state. Pity, would be nice to take them all out in one easy swoop, but life doesn't usually work so smoothly, at least not in typical terms.

One witch raises her head to survey the area and report to her fellow sisters, but a flaming projectile pierces through her ear and cuts those dreams short. The unnamed girl drops to her knees, arrow still impaling her head, causing those immediately next to her to leap up and scatter in a panic.

The hooded figure is too sharp and waits by the log for them all to emerge, brandishing a longsword between two hands and cutting through the first figure that enters into sight directly across the middle, then through the neck to be sure of her death. Several more pour out of hiding, unaware of what happened to the first sister before them. The bodies begin to pile up and release a stench unlike no other, that being the insides of rotten witches.

The attacker removes the cloak that had been shrouding her identity to reveal her face from under the hood. A woman nearing middle-age, eyes withered with deep bags beneath but otherwise adorned by a natural lively beauty that secretly drives the witches crazy with envy.

"Stop her, someone!" the as-of-now head witch shrieks. "One of you useless sisters get her! Don't just run and hide!"

Two shaky witches look at each other then pop out to charge after their guest, unarmed and wholly unprepared. The woman waits for them to arrive closer, then draws her sword back and hacks through one leg of each just below the knee. The witches drop to the ground and screech at frequencies unheard, frantically grasping for their phantom limbs to stop the pain.

"That's too bad, I'm sure it hurts like no other. Poor things," the woman whispers as she grabs each of their calves and tosses them into the massive bonfire still raging.

"You bitch! Our leader is going to liquefy you for mocking us!" one of them shouts as she attempts to stand but falls over onto her stump.

"How strange, I don't see anyone approaching. Better yet, I don't see anyone standing at all to help you. Appears you're on your own." She grabs the loquacious one by the buckled shoe and drags her through the grass while the witch tries to kick with her half-leg. Against the outer wall of the fire, the woman lifts the witch and heaves her into it.

The second witch, thus far quiet, nearly pops her eyes out of her head realizing the fate that awaits. She tries to turn and dig her long and crusted nails into the earth below, but the hooded woman grabs her remaining shoe and overpowers her.

"Wait...WAIT! Aren't you going to let me say any last words?"

"You just wasted your opportunity." The hooded woman lifts the second witch above her head and lobs her into the fire to boil alongside her friend.

Silence falls over the party that just was, with nothing to be heard aside from the blazing flames. Slight footsteps begin to creep toward their hiding spot, as the current witch-in-charge, Belinda, cowers and grips her robes even tighter than before. An ominous figure lands on her position with a thud, causing Belinda to jump a foot into the air with a fright.

"Don't! Leave us be and I will give you anything! Any spell I know, all for you!" Belinda squeals with her hands raised.

"You can't give me what I want, nobody can. All I can do now is settle for second-best." The woman removes a dagger from her cloak and drives it through Belinda's shoulder, holding her in place against the log to bleed out slowly and allow the blade's poisoned coating to do the rest. "You won't want to miss this. I borrowed something from one of your wretched sisters, may she burn in hell." She pulls a small jar from her pocket, holding a clear liquid inside it, and walks toward the rest of the hidden witches, who lay behind another fallen tree.

Belinda opens her mouth to scream and warn the others, yet the mysterious woman moves quickly and smashes the jar on the ground behind the tree trunk. Several witches rise to run away, but fall inside the plume of smoke emitted from the ruptured potion. The woman covers her face so as not to lose consciousness herself, then leaps over the log and swiftly removes several heads with her sword while Belinda watches in horror.

Only five witches remain in sight alive with head, six counting Belinda. The woman drags them out one by one and lays them at the base of a massive oak tree with thick branches overhead. She walks through the darkness to her burlap bag of supplies and removes a sturdy-looking noose made specially for these witches here tonight.

She wraps the knot around the first unfortunate witch on the ground, tossing the long side of the rope over the tall branch and yanking it hard. The sister stands forcefully and gasps for breath with bloodshot eyes, clawing at the noose around her neck as veins begin to bulge and the hue in her face turns from crimson to purple.

"What do you have to say, Sister?" the woman speaks, loosening her grip to lower the witch down to solid ground, but giving it a short tug as a reminder.

"Sister, please! We're innocent!" she wheezes through involuntary tears.

"You're innocent? Out here in the middle of the night, in the middle of the woods being innocent?"

"Yes! Yes, of course! What is it thou believes us to have done?" Sister Margaret slips in dialect, and the cloaked woman only grins ear to ear beneath the luminescence of the full moon.

"Thou? Oh, Sister..." she whispers, pulling a small glass jar from her pocket as Margaret's eyes bulge again for an entirely different reason. "Thou hath committed so many sins, I cannot even begin to recount them here, witch."

She yanks Margaret's head back by the hair and pours the bottle of holy water down her throat, holding her hand over the mouth to force it closed and dropping them both to the ground. Margaret lands on top, while the woman has her unoccupied arm and both legs wrapped around the agonizing witch, staring up at the stars and feeling bliss course through her veins as the holy water delivers its justice to the witch from the inside out.

"Do you feel that?" she whispers in Margaret's ear. "Of course, you do." Blood pours from her nostrils and both corners of her eye sockets, but the woman pays no mind.

"Your suffering is nothing. Your sisters' suffering is nothing," she continues. "I revel in every agonizing second you struggle and wish for death, I eat it up. I eat it right up! If only there was a way to keep you from dying so I could enjoy this longer...I hope you're miserable, wench, but then again I KNOW you are."

Margaret's kicks and jerks devolve to twitches and ticks, then finally stillness. The woman plops her on the ground adjacent then stomps the heel of her boot into the fallen witch's nose.

One remains in place, Mary, seated on a stump and watching the events take place with an empty expression. She doesn't even flinch upon Margaret's facial obliteration, but keeps her eyes trained on the crusader approaching her now.

"You, why haven't you run?" she asks Mary.

"Run where? Where is there to go in this forest? I wouldn't survive until dawn by myself."

"Very well. You wish to die here, then?"

"If it's my turn, yes. Better than dying out there," Mary points to the darkness. "All I request is for you to get it over with as quickly as possible."

She eyes Mary sharply. "You're not evil. You aren't one of them."

"What makes you say that?"

The woman removes another glass bottle from her pocket, pulls out the cork, and flicks a few drops onto Mary's face.

"Why did you do that?"

"This is blessed water. Had no effect on you."

Mary wipes the water from her face and stares at it on her palm. "No. I'm not one of them."

"You shouldn't be here. Now that their ritual has begun, the witches are bound to these grounds until the purpose of the ceremony has been fulfilled. That isn't going to happen. Go, before you can't."

"I don't have anywhere else to go. I lied to Priestess Elizabeth so she would take me in, provide me shelter, teach me skills to survive, but now that is gone too! Why are YOU even here?"

"Keep your voice down. You don't want the others to hear and turn on you."

"Well?!"

"My name is Abigail," she sighs. "Witches, their sisters from another location, took my children to use for a spell, probably killed them. They attacked my home, blindsided my husband and killed him immediately, but left me alive to watch it all happen. One of the witches, though, over-zealous and young, left me within inches of death just for the fun of it. They all have to die, on principle alone, and I'm going to do it. I'm going to kill them all without mercy, and I SHOULD kill you to be on the safe side, but you are someone's daughter too, no matter how lost you are."

"That's…tragic, I'm sorry…but you can't just kill an entire group of people, can you? What if there are some out there like me, who don't want to be there but have no other choice?"

"A worthy price to pay. There will be innocent casualties, although the welfare of the greater good will benefit far more this way. Look at these three," she points to the burlap sacks, "I saved their lives tonight. Had I killed you, that is still a win, three innocents rescued against one lost. No offense."

"No, I get it…fair enough, I can't stop you. It would not have been a complete loss if I was killed, especially to save their lives."

"Whatever you've done, whoever you are, it isn't a drop in the bucket to the evil these creatures have inflicted on their victims and their families," Abigail replies. "Even the worst of us, humans, we aren't capable of falling to the depths of witches. It just isn't in us, that's what makes you one of THEM. They would have found you out soon, you know that? There is a stench they carry, and you don't have it. You may have been able to fake it until now, but not for long."

"One could almost be fooled into thinking tonight was a nice night," Mary speaks after a long silence between them. The sound of a roaring fire blankets the nightscape, crickets and owls echo through cool air. "There are more witches hidden inside that tree trunk. It's hollow, I watched them crawl inside."

Abigail stands with conviction, nods at Mary, and heads toward the log silently. Kneeling next to the opening, she shoots her arm inside to pull out a black buckled shoe attached to a clawing witch. A row of gasps escapes the fateful tube.

"Save me, sisters! Please, help me!"

Abigail drags the struggling witch over rocks and sticks while the others pour out of hiding to scatter in all directions. She lays kicking and screaming on the ground as Abigail grabs the back of her robe, lifts her high into the air, and lobs the sorceress flailing into the fire.

Silence overtakes the area, all witches freezing in position. Warbling shrieks of despair escape the flames, as the witch leaps up to attempt an escape with the skin melting from her face and a putrid off-color smoke filling their sky. Abigail stares with the rest of them, unable to remove their eyes from what may be the fate of nearly everyone still standing within shouting distance. Chilling air, nearly imperceptible to the human psyche, yet the witches break down under the crushing gravity of their hopeless situation.

"Listen up, bitches! My name is Abigail Walker, wife and mother of two. Those three people, my husband and two children, were brutally murdered by a separate sect of your sisters, and as such, this is your responsibility! The pain I have been made to feel has been indescribable and greater than any human should be forced to endure. However, I have great news! You are not human and your suffering will be immense! Welcome to your private hell, sisters, for tonight you are all going to fucking die."

Chaos erupts as the witches still standing tear through the clearing like headless chickens on an errant mission of guideless survival. Mary dashes behind a tree. Abigail closes her eyes and breathes in the adrenaline rush of another sisterhood falling victim to rightful vengeance. Yes…enjoy your last breaths…the final beatings of your hearts before their energy goes dim. The witches are powerless without their most useful asset, time, of which they have little left.

Abigail opens her eyes and glances at the tree hiding Mary, who is poking her head out to witness the slaughter. Pulling two gleaming daggers from her robe, she smirks at Mary and floats into duty, the obligation of a righteous mother done wrong to avenge her fallen family.

The first witch within striking distance succumbs to a knife slice on the side of her neck, dropping to the ground, howling in horror as she presses both hands to the spurting wound. Abigail lifts her into the air and tosses her into the fire beside another smoldering sister.

The second witch, petrified in position like a fear-laden tree stuck in a state of stone, halts in her tracks with mouth agape at the approaching warrior. Two quick cuts and down she goes in a heap of blood secreted from both of her inner thighs.

"Are you frightened? Poor thing! You look terrified, probably very similar to how my daughter looked, wishing for her mother. I couldn't be there for her, but I'm here now, and your pain will be over in seconds." The second witch is propelled into the inferno, growing exponentially with each enchantress it consumes. The yellow and orange hue takes on a blue and greenish sheen.

The third, fourth, and fifth witches are vaulted into their burning tombs, flailing as they land on a pile of charred and ashen corpses. Witch number six puts up a fight, attempting a spell upon Abigail as she approaches, but ultimately succumbs like the rest as her organs are forcefully penetrated several times by both silver daggers before she is able to recite the words. The same smell secreted from the fire now invades Abigail's nostrils again, although she can't be sure if it is coming from the stab wounds or cinders.

Six shivering witches remain standing meekly in a half-circle around Abigail, who sheaths one of the daggers to form a fist, holding firm in her position. The first sorceress loses her nerve and screams, charging toward the scorned mother with reckless abandon. Abigail deftly sidesteps and hammers the dagger down through the top of the skull while the witch gurgles mindlessly. She rips the knife from the head and angrily drills it behind the ear for good measure.

"Next?"

One of the witches, the one who appears to be youngest, begins to weep and runs for the dark woods away from the safety of their massive carcass fire.

"Sister! No!" the eldest witch warns, but she is too late. The rookie runs headlong into the enchanted barrier and evaporates into a cloud of drizzling sanguinary soot and sinewy tissue raining down on the bewitched territory.

Each of the four sisters drops to their knees in a panic, trembling too heavily to move any further. Abigail walks to the fallen which is closest and lets her off easy; she slits her throat and yanks her neck nearly completely around.

The second witch, a bit less so, is stabbed through each of her closed and sobbing eyes before having a wooden stake driven into her vacuous heart. Abigail tidies the area by dragging them both to the fire, but leaves them laying at the edge of the flames to burn slowly.

"As for you," she says to the third witch, who drops to her hands and knees before her.

"Please! I beg of you mercy, Sister!"

"Sister...did you or your sisters show my children mercy when you slaughtered them like animals?" she seethes, driving the dagger between the begging witch's ribs, who's shrieks escalate tenfold. "Or my husband, did you serve him with the dignity a righteous man deserves? Did you allow him to pray a final time to make peace with his Lord?"

Abigail's hand shakes while her breathing intensifies. Mary stares from the tree still, in disbelief of what she is hearing. How can such a fair woman carry such rage? Is she part demon? This unexpected visitor could have ended Mary with the rest, yet took pity on her for possessing a neutral spirit. Did she see potential in the young wanderer to do good, or had she simply not been tainted yet?

"I know what we'll do, yes. You are already in position for it, so shouldn't be a big deal. We are going to say a prayer together for my husband and children to bid them safe passage and hope they find peace."

"NO! Anything else, I beg you!"

"Yes...repeat after me."

"I can't, it's...it will be too agonizing!"

"You do not know pain until you face the wrath of a vengeful mother, sister, this is only the Lord's penance. Now, repeat after me," Abigail demands. "Our Father which art in Heaven."

"Our Father," she winces through anguish, "which art in...I can't!"

"Say it."

"It is too painful!"

"Say it!" Abigail shoves her face into the dirt, grasping her hair.

"Heaven," the young witch mutters, muffled and pained.

"Our Father which art in Heaven, Hallowed be thy name."

"Hallowed be thy name."

"Thy kingdom come. Thy will be done in earth," Abigail whispers.

"Thy kingdom come. Thy will be done-" the witch gurgles as Abigail stomps on the back of her neck and wrenches it upward by a handful of hair. The snap of the spinal cord rings throughout the forest and she releases the head to splat into the dirt beneath.

"How foolish of you to think I would allow you within even an inch of salvation. I am not holy, I do not forgive. Burn."

Abigail drags the witch by the hair and back of the cloak then heaves her too into the open flame, which is now blazing higher than it has so far. After what felt like an entire night of hunting, she inhales deeply and exhales through her nose, staring up at the luminescent stars for clarity. Mary was right, it is a beautiful evening.

Only one wench remaining of an entire coven. A successful mission by anyone's standards, although there is still work to do, so much work and it is time to be traveling on to the next.

"Witch! You are the only one still breathing!"

The lone survivor attempts to sink even further into the earth, sobbing and shaking for she had been forced to witness each sister's demise before, breathing in the pungent stench of their burning essence. Abigail stomps over and kicks her onto her back.

"Stand up and look into my eyes," she commands.

The witch rises weakly as she is told, staring into the deep and gray eyes of the woman above her.

"My name is Abigail Walker, as you may have heard before. What's my name?"

"Abigail."

"Abigail what?"

"Abigail Walker," the witch wheezes.

"You remember that, Abigail Walker and what happened here tonight?"

"You k-killed our entire coven."

"Yes, I did. Everyone except you and Mary, by design. You are going to run to your leader, whoever that is, but you are going to find someone ranked higher than yourself and you will tell her what happened here. Tell her I'm coming for her too. Tell her I will do the same to her coven, I will kill everyone there, then move on again and again until you are all dead. You won't know when it will happen, yet you will always wonder right up until the second it is too late. Now go! I release you from your oath!" she shouts, kicking the witch in the backside. "See you soon."

The witch scurries through the carnage and disappears into darkness, carrying the message to her distant sisters. Another job well done. Scalded witches and scattered bodies, thus for tonight, the world is a safer place. Abigail sits on a log and ponders these events before taking a big stretch and opting to walk away at last.

"You're just going to leave me?" Mary clamors as she runs from behind her tree of safety.

"Haven't left yet, have I?"

"You were about to!"

"I don't have any business left here," Abigail answers as she straightens herself up in preparation.

"You WERE going to leave me!"

"Leave you here where you belong? Yes, I was. You're a lost soul, who some would still consider a child. I don't have a life left, this IS my life now."

"And what do I have? I never wanted to be here, but once I was *accused* of being a witch in town, what other option did I have? No trial, no jury, only public opinion that Mary is a witch and should be hung with the others. I have nothing. I am nobody," Mary relinquishes. "Let me help you. I know, and you know, you will not survive forever living a life like this."

"Never crossed my mind."

"I'm serious. Let me help you."

"I'm not sure you have the fortitude for it. And to trust you in the heat of a siege? What if you fail me then? How do I know you have the stomach for it?" Abigail chastises.

One of the fallen witches stirs and claws into the dirt to propel herself forward, painstakingly inch by inch. Mary marches over commandingly and stomps her heel into the wounded witch's head, caving it in, all while staring at Abigail stone-faced.

Neither of them moves. The bonfire rages in the background. Abigail bursts into laughter staring at Mary's display of commitment, her foot still stuck inside the witch's skull.

"Fair enough, I need someone around whom I can trust. Go ahead and start tossing the rest of the bodies into the flames while I load up and set these people free. I'll help you finish when I'm done."

"They'll never know what hit them."

XIX
You Only Die Once

"**H**ere it is, Bradley, I finally got my hands on one."

"How? I heard these were impossible to get, and they check your ID too!"

"Saved up my allowance and gave it to my older brother. He bought it for us, but I had to swear I wouldn't tell anybody. He would beat my ass for even telling YOU."

"I won't tell, Rickey. I swear too."

"Yeah, well I already promised my brother and you see how much that was worth. Don't tell anybody."

"I won't."

"Swear!"

"I swear, okay? Pinky promise, cross my heart and hope to die, all of it. Why would I get us in trouble when I want to play too?"

"Okay…fine," Rickey concedes, removing the cardboard box from the larger box he used for transport.

Bradley brushes the red and black glossy box top with his two primary fingers. "You Only Die Once…I didn't expect the game to be this big."

"Be careful with that, would you? It also costs a lot more than you would expect, and I had to borrow money from my brother just to get it. You don't even know how many allowances I still have to give him, plus interest."

"What's interest?"

"I don't know, but he said I wouldn't like it."

Rickey and Bradley carefully crack the seal around the board game lid and lift it from the base. The bottom slides down with a squeak and finally pops free as the two boys slowly turn and stare at one another with glee.

"Don't let me ruin your kiss. What are you dorks up to now?" Andrea, Bradley's nosy and annoying older sister, sneaks behind them. Bradley nervously throws the bag back on top of the box to hide it.

"Hi, Andrea. I thought it smelled like stupid in here," Rickey retorts.

"Get out of here, Andrea! We're playing a game and you're only going to ruin it."

"You don't trust your cool big sister?"

"No!" they bark in unison.

"I'm not your sister, dweeb," she flicks Rickey's ear.

"You can be my girlfriend, though," he mutters back.

"What?"

"Nothing."

"Okay, thanks for stopping by, Andrea. You've overstayed your welcome already," Bradley dismisses.

"I know you're doing something weird in here…but whatever." She turns and leaves the room, shutting the door behind her.

They sit still for a moment waiting for her to jump back in and surprise them, but nothing comes. Silence, anticipation. Worry.

"Good going, man! Now she's going to tell on us!" Rickey complains.

"She isn't going to call your brother. She didn't even see the game, so calm down."

"Let's just get to this, yeah? It's been a long enough wait."

Bradley removes the bag from atop the game and they resume where they left off, eager to begin and incredulous it is finally happening. Inside the box lies at least a hundred pieces requiring assembly.

"What do they think I am, some kind of architect?" Rickey blabbers.

"The architect would have drawn the finished design. All we have to do is follow the instructions, bozo."

"Whatever, smartass. Well, go ahead and build it, Da Vinci!"

"I'm working on it. Here's the instruction book," Bradley tails off, already deep in thought.

"This is just great! First, we had to wait forever to even get the game, then I had to get my brother involved just to buy it, and NOW we can't even play it right away!"

"Shut up and help me. This could either take a long time, or you could pitch in and cut that in half."

And so the boys built the board game, following directions closely with a few mistakes along the way, as well as a lot of bickering and a couple curse words. What stood before them was a massive display unlike any board game Rickey or Bradley had ever seen.

"Woah…" they both whisper, stepping back and staring in awe of their handiwork.

"It's huge," Rickey whispers.

"Unbelievable," Bradley murmurs.

The game features a large devil face in front of a Ferris wheel, red lights that actually plug into the socket, circus tent, and painted-on fire displays, among other things surrounding a three-dimensional game track circling the massive tent. The color palette features a palpable theme that screams red. They notice there are no cards or other pieces, only command prompts inscribed on the spaces themselves.

"How do we play?" Rickey asks.

"I'm looking through that right now. It says 'Welcome to the Carnival of Nefarious Intent. Enter the tent at your own great peril! The cost of loss will be dire.' That's all they have."

"Nefarious? Whatever, just spin the wheel in the middle. It can't be that complicated if the idiots we know at school have played it."

"True," Bradley replies, spinning the wheel to land on three. His character moves three spaces on its own.

"Whoa," they mumble in unison again, staring at each other.

Through trial and error, the boys make it to the top of the carnival tent after facing inopportune challenges commanded by the game, such as punching a fellow contender in the face. Bradley was happy to oblige.

"Six more spaces to reach the end, and every one of them says to return back to start. How the hell do we win if the wheel only goes to six?" Rickey complains, lightly rubbing his jaw.

"Don't be a sore loser, just try it out."

So Rickey does, spinning a lucky six, yet falling one space short of victory and watching his character tumble down the side of the tent and settling back at start.

"You're kidding me, this game is stupid! It's rigged so nobody can even win it!"

"Just try again, there must be some sort of mistake?"

"I don't have enough time tonight, I need to get home. We can try again another day, I guess, I don't know. So much time for nothing," Rickey shakes his head.

"Alright, well I'm going to leave the game just like this, that way we don't have to waste hours of setup next time."

"Sounds good. See you at school." Rickey slings his backpack over his shoulder, grabs his skateboard, and almost swings the door into the eaves-dropping Andrea, who ducks into the bathroom adjacent.

Several hours pass and Bradley can't keep his eyes off the display in the corner of his room. Homework was a disaster to complete, and even during his nightly shower, all he could think about was how to surmount those final six spaces. It's only a riddle, he thought to himself, an obstacle with a hidden solution. He would definitely need to be the one to solve the puzzle. No offense to Rickey.

Now lying in bed, two hours past the time he should have been to sleep on a school night, those excited thoughts roll through the threshold of enjoyment and take hold of his nerves. The devil face, with a grin so cartoonish yet evil, remains painted behind his eyelids while sleep remains as elusive as that winning space in the game.

Whenever he discovers the secret, Bradley decides he doesn't want to share it. Let Rickey squirm for answers. Even if he found out, he's such a loud mouth that the entire school would know by the end of the week. Staying up all night to solve the issue has to be worth something.

Feeling himself slip into the next stage of relaxation for the first time tonight, Bradley feels the grow of red light upon his face. This must be the consequences of obsessing over the game, he hopes, although it doesn't go away with time.

Finally, he opens an eye for the peace of mind and inspects their sinister board game, but finds it to be dark and inanimate in the room's corner, exactly the way it was left. The blurriness of middle-of-the-night eyes wears off and Bradley finally sees well enough to recognize a dull reddish hue blanketing the rest of the room. He forces his eyes shut as hard as he can to avoid the confrontation of truth. It's an illusion, you're tired, you played the game for too long, all things he repeats neurotically to try and get to sleep. This is normal, everything is fine.

Faint carnival music rises to his ears in the dark, but nobody plugged in the game for it to play? Yet, when he points his ear toward it with eyes still shut, it is easy to recognize that the sounds are not emanating from there. Bradley buries his face into the pillow to escape this augmented reality, yet all he gets in return is the crescendo of circus music.

Flashing red lights distract his attempts to relax and he bolts upright in bed, unable to ignore this any further. Carnival tunes and clown horns swirl his surroundings and cause him to feel a seasickness in the form of being overwhelmed by sensation. This is all his fault for playing the game, yet the board is silent and dark?! That demon face remains grinning, even cutting through the low visibility of luminescent red light flooding the room. The source seems to be beneath his bed, light and music and all. Bradley can't take it any more...

"MOM!!! DAD!!!"

He resorts to the instincts of pre-consciousness, even as a budding teen, although where else could he turn? After a brief moment, their dormant parental instincts activate to care for young children throughout the night, and his father bursts through the bedroom door, followed by his mother, and then Andrea after a brief pause.

"Bradley?! You scared us half to death, what's going on in here?"

He has the quilt pulled up to his eyes in embarrassment, but points downward and rambles in mumbled speech, "it's my bed, something bad is happening under my bed!"

"Oh, goodness, Bradley," his mother sighs.

"I thought we were over this stage, Bradley?" his father groans. Both parents survey the room, now dark and silent, yet find nothing of note.

"It's that game, I saw him and Rickey playing it earlier!" Andrea snitches, pointing excitedly toward the board game in the corner.

"Where the hell did you get that?" Dad asks.

"Rickey brought it over, but I heard something, I swear! Music and red lights!"

"Now, Bradley, you know how you get sometimes…we've come so far in dealing with this," Mom relents.

"Please, just look under my bed then I will go to sleep in peace and we can laugh about this tomorrow. Please."

Mom and Dad share a look and both shrug their shoulders.

"If it will make you feel better, Bradley, fine. I will look under your bed for monsters, but you have to go to sleep after. Promise?"

"Promise."

"Okay, then," Dad groans as he slowly drops to his hands and knees.

Mom wanders over to the board game without Bradley noticing to inspect the sinister contraption.

Dad lifts the sheet to poke his head underneath, followed by both shoulders as he pats around to feel for lurking villains.

Mom eyes the instruction booklet and brings it close to her face so she can read it in the dim light. "You Only Die Once?"

Bradley's eyes nearly bulge from his skull, feeling as though he has been caught, turning to stare blankly at his mother.

She thumbs through the book with eyes squinted, before finally flipping it over entirely. The back page is inscribed with black lettering that she must once again pull close to her face to read. "Just Kidding."

The red lights and music from beneath the bed kick on while Dad has only his bottom half hanging out.

"What the fu-" he shouts as the music peaks again and he is sucked into the void.

"Welcome to the show, may you never leave again!" a charismatic voice clamors from unseen origins with a twisted laugh. "Nothing you do can help you now, so sit back and enjoy the ride!"

Bradley's dad is swallowed down a red slide into the depths while he screams in terror at what he knows is an irreversible fate. The same devil's face, now twenty-times larger, cackles maniacally at his misfortune while jesters ring the buffoon tune. Balloons inflate of his friends' and family's heads, only dead, all around as a rollercoaster of souls circles endlessly about his position.

"Caleb!" his wife shouts from above, as he begs and pleads her not to follow.

Clawed hands grasp her soft digits and yank her down the same ill-fated slide that landed her husband in this pit.

"This is all your fault! You and your dipshit friend killed Mom and Dad!" Andrea chastises her brother, who tries to hide in bed.

"I didn't…it wasn't…" he stammers, out of excuses but searching for anything to hide his own disappointment.

A slow-moving and slick hand bounds outward from his bed frame, target set on Andrea's ankle. It grasps her tightly and yanks, smacking her head on the floor and rendering her defenseless. Down goes Andrea, into the depths, eyes closed and silent for once in Bradley's life.

He sits in his bed, frozen in fear and ashamed at his own inaction. What should he do? What could he have done? Shivering he remains among the flashing red lights and jovial carnival hymns.

"This is the show we've been waiting for!" the unnamed voice cackles in a frenzy. "Three fresh souls to sacrifice in our game, three free spaces we grant thee in vain."

Bradley leaps from his bed out of compulsion and runs to the game. A 'return to start' space disappears as his father screams in agony from deep below his bed. His hand floats toward the spinning wheel, having been so close to the end, but stops as he hears his dear mother shout once again. Another space dissolves into nothing, a blank square like the others.

Finally, Andrea shrieks out her anguish, causing another of the barricade spaces to fade. Bradley stares in disbelief after sitting up all night wondering how to solve the puzzle. Then, he has his answer.

He gawks at the game for a full minute, yet three more 'return to start' spaces remain in place. He MIGHT be able to pass those, but the journey had been fraught with nearly-missed terrors, like orders that would directly lead to his own harm or worse. Maybe finishing the game would bring his family members back?

Bradley picks up the instructions again and reads the cover aloud. "You Only Die Once," followed by the back, "Just Kidding." That could only mean they have died but will be revived and theoretically able to die again, or so hopes the idealistic young mind of a freshly-made orphan. By all accounts, he has just about zero else left to lose aside from his own life.

Fighting back tears for his departed parents, he tries to make sense once more of the game, though distracted by blurred vision and brain fog. Six spaces. Three gone and three remain. Primordial synapses fire with the efficacy of striking wet matches. Family dead, bad. Must fix. He can even trick himself into mourning Andrea for the time being if it helps the cause.

The sounds of a raging carnival party and amusement park rides lingers from beneath the bed, though buried deep and drowned out by the task at hand. Three spaces remain, but three were removed, one for each sacrificial soul. An idea forms at the snap of a finger in Bradley's mind and coincides with the blowing of a horn in the depths.

He pulls out his phone and dials Rickey. It must be at least two in the morning, though his brain did not register the time.

"Are you kidding me?"

"Rickey. How are your parents? Your brother?"

"I'm sure they're all doing lovely and sleeping, like I was doing, and like you should be doing!"

"Go wake them up," Bradley suggests, turning to look at his bed and seeing the red light finally fade away. "Something bad is about to happen to you, but it's a good thing, trust me. Wake them up and get them in your room, you will all know what to do from there. Make sure you get your brother too. I figured it out, Rickey. It only took me all night, but I figured out how to beat the game. Just TRUST ME, okay?" he emphasizes with his eyes on those final three spaces.

XX

Float Like a Butterfly

I had a dream last night, but it was about today. I dreamt that today would be the actual dream and my sleep was reality, which is odd because the day has transpired exactly as I foresaw, like how a dream should play out though much more boring. Such a level of predictability is stressful in a life dictated by chaos. I don't like it at all.

So I went to bed to start fresh, escape the day and leave it where it should lay; yesterday. I lounged in bed, falling asleep, waking up, asleep, awake, asleep, awake. Eventually, I became cognizant of the fact I went under because my previous day, of which I hoped to escape, began to replay scene for scene like a rerun of an old television series I had seen a hundred times.

The trance of slumber started to lighten, a sign I would soon rise, though internally I rushed the process along to escape the second-telling of my uncomfortable day. Only, I remained stuck in the moment of boredom and unable to move forward and begin the next day. Nobody was around, nothing appeared normal, thus it must have been a dream.

Finally, and without much warning, I realized the clouds had parted, so to speak. Consciousness. Awareness. In a different location to boot, but mentally lagging from the restless night of sleep. I never used to dream, or remember them, and each morning was glorious because of it. The sleep of the dead, awaking fresh and primed to ignite like a powder keg, seize the day sort of thing. At last, a new beginning. Clarity to power through my negativity and leave it behind in my multiple yesterdays.

That night I hoped to recharge the batteries a bit with old movies and television shows. Let the brain vegetate and heal itself, think of nothing and fall into a deep sleep. Maybe I might even be able to have a GOOD dream tonight, goodness knows I've been lacking in those. This brings me to my present moment.

What a fantastic sitcom I found for myself, one I used to watch religiously as a child and therefore the memories are beyond pleasant. It also happens to be an overnight marathon, just what the doctor ordered, that and a tall glass of cognac for good measure.

The alarm clock rings on the table beside me, sitting next to my empty glass and interrupting my show. The ethereal trance in which I had been floating is broken by the chatter of the bell, an annoyance I could do without. Why did I set the alarm for my bedtime instead of the time to rise for work?

The time reads 6:30 am, though my mind refuses to accept it. I know I have watched a few episodes now, but not eleven hours' worth?! The red block numbers burn into my irises, though they don't make any sense. It isn't half past six in the morning no matter how you spin it. It just isn't. Stress is the culprit here, so I set the alarm for 6:40 just to be sure, then return to my glorious show. Perhaps I should go to sleep after this episode anyway, although…two more thirty-minute episodes elapse before the alarm rings again. How did I watch an hour of television in ten minutes? How is it 6:40 in the morning?

Did I dream the entire marathon? My wish was for pleasant dreams and it doesn't get much more cheerful than that, though my confusion mounts higher when I finally capitulate by getting dressed and notice the same TV show is playing. People talk about those twilight sleeps where you get trapped between planes, which might be what happened, what's been happening for several nights. Tonight, when I get home, it's time to resort to heavy measures.

Which I did, five minutes ago now and the effects are reaching around my body like a warm and heavy blanket. Two pills meant for relaxation dropped into a large glass of cognac like acid reflux effervescents. Not medically advisable, as labeled on the pill bottle, though it sure is effective. It feels as though the day passed so quickly, it never happened at all, like I left my comfortable bed and walked a circle straight back to it.

To test my cognizance, I thoroughly inspect my alarm clock for discrepancies against what I believe to be true. 8:30 pm, checks out. It's dark outside now and believable that it could be soon nearing nine at night. My eyes grow unbearably heavy and tonight I opt to turn off the TV and get the most of my deep sleep.

Head hits the pillow hard, though I sit up again quickly to have a sip of water before hibernation, and notice the reflecting glow from the screen surrounds me even though I just shut it off. Friday night, so no alarm, though I should set it regardless to make sure I don't sleep fourteen hours to compensate for lack of rest recently. It's been one minute, so 8:31, all is right. Does that say AM next to it? I just slept for twelve hours plus one minute?

I leap from bed and frantically run about the house for answers, which only confuses me further after seeing light pouring through my windows. How, what, why, all questions burrowing into my consciousness in repetitive succession. Yes, how indeed? What happened? Why is it morning? Then the epiphany hits me.

I must be dreaming now? One thing is for certain, that being that I JUST laid my head down but did NOT sleep for twelve hours plus one minute.

I exist inside a dream with full consciousness and sobriety, although perhaps the latter not for long. Living a life without consequences, our every wish since childhood, now manifesting with taking large chugs from a bottle of cognac. What bad could happen in a dream? Who wouldn't want the ability to drink as much as they want with zero repercussions?

Who should I rob? Might I even kill? Every wildly evil impulse I ever suppressed floods my senses now that they may be real possibilities to commit. Living in a dream, yet how many days in this recent streak of oddities have also been my imagination? How can I be positive beyond a shadow of a doubt that any day I have ever existed actually happened? My thoughts sour under the ambiguity of disbelief. I might not even be real. Everyone I ever met could be a fallacy of an imagination run amuck. I may be alone and shackled inside the pit of my own creation, or I could exist as a sacrificial lamb in another's world. We don't know. I don't know. Meaning as I know it is crumbling before me like a structure made of paper and soaked in water.

"Who gives a fuck? Nothing is real!" I shout to the whole world, meaning me, as I guzzle the remnants of my trusty cognac bottle practically fused with my hand and gas the truck in reverse down the driveway. A little old man walking his dog decides to cross my sidewalk at an inopportune time and I plow him over like a rabid bull. Never fear, for not even in my wildest dreams would I ever fantasize about harming a dog, so I scoop the good boy up into the cab and zoom down the road as if I was a renegade monster truck driver crushing everything in my path.

Running over parked cars, dropped skateboards, and blowing through mailboxes, I'm a man flying down an open highway with no speed limit nor law enforcement in sight. What else could I do? Impulse control is now about as real as the air I breathe into my nose in this truck made of my own nightmarish imagination.

Sanity fades for lack of needing it, and I demolish the next pedestrian I see. How fun! Swerving from sidewalk to sidewalk, every walker on the street meets their end at the hands of my grille. This is the most fun dream I have ever been a part of, with the good fortune to be sitting behind the driving wheel, both literally and otherwise. I also happened to have racked up over a thousand points on the road. The last unfortunate walker met his end after I launched my truck off the back of a four-door sedan and landed on him while he fetched the morning paper. The downside being I rolled the truck in the process but didn't feel a thing thanks to the dreamscape! Or maybe the cognac, possibly both.

I crawl out of my burning four-wheel-drive and float down the street, still walking on physical feet but otherwise blissfully strolling. My street I have lived on for years, some of my neighbors whom I have tried to avoid at the mailbox…this avenue now lays in shambles, crushed and aflame but fixable the moment I wake up again. What a phenomenon! Burn the world and leave it for dead until I awake again to harmonious life. I can't help but laugh, though, at the sight of old man Marvin smashed on the sidewalk with tire marks on his robe and skin. Is it impolite to notify a neighbor you killed him in a dream? Another pedestrian walks down the street at a half-jogging pace.

"Hello, friend! Do you have a car close by that I can use?"

"To use? I'm not just going to give you-" he finishes, cut short by a haymaker to the jaw that knocks him out cold while I belly-laugh over his comatose body.

"This is my world, pal," I add, digging through his pockets and taking car keys. I click the red alarm button to pinpoint the car's location and walk toward it. Nice ride, a sports car that easily takes me one hundred, one twenty, then a hundred and forty miles per hour through this single-lane residential street. The carefree thrill is exhilarating to say the least, I have never felt less chained and possibly because this is the first time I have ever been literally without a care.

A few unlucky houses devolve into pieces. I let go of the wheel of the car and close my eyes, gas pedal to the floor below. Not caring feels fantastic. It is impossible for the conscious human mind to fathom a complete lack of consequence or control, though many will claim to know. I am the god of my own existence, a great white shark in a paltry pond. The creation of life for my amusement and destruction is palpable for me, at least in this world. I was not a particularly powerful man in life, yet in here, I am the cosmos. The alpha, theta, sigma, and omega are all my whims and will, as well as everything in between those values.

I will not grab the wheel again. I will not remove my foot from the accelerator, nor will I depress the brakes. I am a control freak in the real world, neurotic over every divisible detail until the minutiae of decision is too diluted to interpret clearly. I am responsible for horrible decisions and even worse outcomes. I have damaged relationships and relinquished opportunities for lesser prospects. No more. Control is given to the universe, which is to say myself while in this state. Take my hand and guide me through my own mire.

The truck crashes through white picket fences and front yard fountains, over flower gardens and vacated children's toys. My mind refuses to manufacture entities without intent to kill them, and thus the world is empty. Another upturned lawn, another skimmed parked car. My vehicle and I are on a one-way drive to wherever that may be.

A cliff approaches as my position shifts to an uphill climb. I open my eyes to observe this change, but see only white horizons in all directions. A blank canvas of a world to my eyes until my brain paints the details. Typically, unless I am incorrect, going up must mean down comes next. Nothing is real beyond a shadow of a doubt, and certainly not this rollercoaster I find myself riding.

Suddenly, the incline plateaus, then dissolves beneath my tires. Might it be the cognac again? But I open an eye regardless just to see my surroundings disappearing while in free fall. I have felt this way a thousand times before, falling through a dream, yet always waking just as I would be nearing the ground. It's coming, I can see it now.

This dreamscape has been enjoyable, though I have destroyed enough to reach a level of boredom. Any second I will wake. Nothing has meaning in this realm, not even fun anymore. In that respect, I am ready to rise. Must be about to happen, the ground is danger-ously close now. I close my eyes to facilitate the manifestation of a jump back to reality, yet nothing happens for several seconds, and then it does. It does happen, like a jolt through my body and stronger than I remember. Sharp pins puncturing my body and head smashing into several things, but I am awake…sort of.

My eyes flutter open to see flames dancing for only a brief second before they close again and stay that way. I am floating underwater, only there isn't a drop in sight. I can feel the cold of the murky depths encasing me within myself in a blanket of my own skin, yet the darkness isn't from lack of light. I cannot hear a sound, senses clouded by the atmospheric weight of the surface overhead and the cavernous depths beneath. This is my dream world, my manufactured oneirological existence I seem destined to be trapped within.

Suddenly the memories of decades gone by play like a film reel of my life's greatest hits, however many of them happened inside my dreams. Nearly half, in fact. How can I be certain which half was which at this point? Neither seems more plausible than the other. Life's happiest moments may have never existed outside my own mind.

Which state am I floating in now? I believed myself to be waking from sleep, which would put me in reality at the present moment, although…what if the opposite is true? Might I have been sleeping before and unconscious after a crash? The thought is sobering, to say the least.

My eyes open with a jolt. The flames are gone. My truck is gone. Whether I have awakened from a dream, or fallen from consciousness into this state does not matter now. I feel good. I feel light, like I had great sleep before or am sleeping presently. There is nowhere else I would rather be than this moment now.

XXI
Lake Umbra

"Is there no moon tonight?" Sharon asks, peering inquisitively through the windshield.

"There is, but it's tiny and I only know because I've been staring that direction for most of the night. Look, over here," Tony points to the far corner of his side of the windshield, a stretch for Sharon to see. "You see that little sliver? Right there, it's about to be covered by that cloud."

"Yes, I see it better now that we turned a bit."

Madison and Doug sit quietly in the back seat, having had more than their fill of fun already, both rather inebriated.

"There's power in a crescent moon, you know," Tony continues. "Many spooky stories like to use a full moon for imagery, but even that small of a crescent carries much more mystique, unless you're talking about werewolves, that is."

"I wasn't, no. Are you writing a ghost story now? Should I be worried?"

"Depends. It IS pretty dark out there. The atmosphere would be perfect for such a story. How do you view yourself in that scenario? A victim? Or survivor?"

"Better than YOU, loser," she mocks. "You would be the idiot that panics and runs into the darkness, never to be seen again. Actually, you would probably attract the ghost right to you as you run away, screaming of course, THEN never to be seen again, but also leaving the three of us perfectly safe. So, thanks." Sharon sarcastically places a hand on his shoulder.

"Are YOU writing a ghost story now? Fair enough, although you aren't pretty enough to be the final girl. You would be lucky to die first and get it over with."

She punches him in the arm, causing the car to jerk. "Some boyfriend you are."

Doug bounces off his seat and hits the floor. "Woah, take it easy, drunk driver!"

"I'm not drunk, you are," Tony fires back.

"Oh yeah, we are." Doug and Madison snort laugh at his joke and obnoxiously carry on for too long.

"What do you say, Sharon? Should we go and find some fun? Even though you almost turned us into a ghost story ourselves."

"Well," she defends, "I'm not ugly, you're ugly."

"You are ugly, bro," Doug comments between them with an arm resting on each chair. "But did I hear you're looking for ghosts? I know this may be hard to believe, but I'm something of an expert on the subject, myself."

"That's up to Sharon," Tony answers, looking back and forth between his girlfriend and the road.

"Sure, whatever, I mean I don't really believe in this stuff anyway. But I'm not going to be the party pooper."

"Nice," Doug whispers. "Coming up in about a mile now, take a right turn onto an old dirt road and park."

"When?"

"I'll tell you when. Just keep straight, like a mile or so."

"This is going to be so rad," the wasted Madison adds.

"You know everything about this, so then you've been here before? What happened?" Tony asks.

"Nothing happened. My source tells me you have to have multiple people, it doesn't work if you come alone. Turn right here."

"Jesus!" Tony exclaims, stomping on the brakes and swerving right.

"So, anyway, there's a bottomless lake right on the other side of this dirt road."

"That doesn't make any sense, Doug, something can't be just like…WITHOUT a bottom. It would pour out the other side of Earth," Madison argues.

"It just means they never found it. And stop interrupting me, because I was getting there. Shut up, or whatever," he giggles drunkenly. "Yeah so anyway, there's a fisherman supposedly. Some people say they see the souls that have drowned, as well."

"Why a fisherman? Seems random for a lake," Tony muses.

"Legend is he was a deep-sea fisherman who owned this land. One night he heard some college-age kids out here swimming, probably doing drugs or drinking. You know, or whatever. They ended up drowning and he dove in trying to save them, but didn't resurface for twenty-four hours. Now he patrols the area every night and drowns anyone on his property as a sort of revenge," he chuckles.

They drive past a private property sign and the car comes to a long screeching halt down the dirt road.

"What the hell are you doing, Tony?" Sharon shouts.

"This isn't a game, Doug! I'm not going to risk all of our lives to chase thrills in the middle of the night!"

"Chill out, Tony. I thought you were into it, you know?"

"I thought it might be fun, yeah, but this isn't the same as saying a name into a mirror three times or messing around with a Ouija board. We're on his property now and you're telling me he drowns anyone he finds here?"

"Babe, it's just a myth," Sharon comforts. "Every small town has them, they're all for fun. It's ridiculous, if anything."

"That's fine, and I like ghost stories, but I'm more concerned with getting us all home safely. I made a mistake, I'm willing to admit it. Let's get home now and just be done with it." Tony puts the car in reverse, but the back-tire spins without traction in the loose dirt and they stay stuck in place.

"You're a real bummer, dude," Madison laughs.

Tony ignores her quip and reaches into the glove compartment to grab his flashlight, staring sternly at Sharon. He climbs out of the car to inspect their situation.

"What's wrong with your boyfriend, Sharon?" she continues.

"Yeah, he's being a real sissy all of the sudden," Doug echoes.

"MY boyfriend? The man who got your sorry drunken asses home tonight and a dozen nights before this? The man who never asks for anything but always takes care of everyone? That guy?"

"Don't get your panties in a bunch," Doug whispers weakly, looking at Madison for support.

"Whatever," Sharon replies, getting out of the car to help Tony.

The couple sits in the back seat, buzzed and exhausted, but comfortable enough to relax in their present situation.

"Tony? Where are you?" she asks.

"I'm over here, trying to get signal." He waves the flashlight to guide her.

"What are we going to do now? Do you need my help?"

"There's a nail in the tire," Tony responds. "We have a flat and I can't call anyone out here."

"Can't you change it? Hell, even I know how to do it."

"Yes, I know how to change a tire, but Doug doesn't keep a spare, apparently. Would you expect anything different?"

"Oh, Tony. You're so responsible, why do you keep such dumbass friends?" she guffaws into the black night air.

"I wish I had a solid answer for you. Let's walk back toward the main road a bit until we can dial out. They'll probably be asleep in there."

"Lead the way, you're the one with the flashlight. You know there's nothing to worry about, Tony. You know that, right?"

"Yeah, I know. It just crossed through my mind this is a stupid idea, regardless. Like what are we hoping to achieve either way?" Tony continues onward with his trusty flashlight shining the way as they walk for several minutes and nearly hit the main road.

"What's that on the floor up there? That ain't dirt, it looks shiny."

He continues pointing the light ahead of them and aimed toward the floor. "Nails. They're nails."

Thousands of them in a wide row stretching across the entire dirt road. Sharon kicks the massive pile. "It's a miracle we only lost one tire."

"Sharon. You can't seriously be making jokes right now? It's obvious this was placed here deliberately as a trap! This isn't the same thing as someone just dropping a box of nails!"

"Keep your voice down if you're so worried about it. Yes, I agree with you. This was done for a purpose, but probably as a deterrent, not to murder us. We *are* on private property, Tony. I wouldn't want people driving through my backyard, either."

"I get you're a logical person, but that's taking it a bit far, don't you think? Maybe if there was only a 'No Trespassing' sign, I might agree with you more," Tony argues.

"Fine, but what do we do now? We have to be halfway to the road now, so do we continue on or go back and get them?"

"Would be smarter to go out and make the call first to make sure help is on its way. I just feel kind of weird about leaving them trapped in the middle of nowhere."

"I know you do, so let's go get them and come back. We'll be out on the road all together in less than fifteen minutes and we can wait for help there. That is, unless Doug and Madison are already dead," Sharon deadpans.

"Why do I date you?"

"I'm the best you can get, that's why. Let's go get your idiot friend and his moronic girlfriend. Seriously, everything's fine."

"Yeah, well I'm the one who listened to that idiot and drove us out here," Tony laments. "I keep thinking I'm hearing sounds too, but it must just be the countryside playing tricks on me."

"I haven't heard anything. You're cracking up, Mr. Tony, the exposure is getting to you. Look, shine the flashlight over there. I can faintly see the car."

"Great, let's grab them and go."

Tony and Sharon continue carefully through the hidden pitfalls of desert landscape in darkness. All is quiet, as would be expected, yet the set of circumstances and Tony's heightened awareness have cast a watchful eye over their position. An invasive and foreboding eye, at that.

"Hand me the flashlight, I think I see Doug sitting in the back seat," Sharon requests, taking it from Tony and shining the low beam through the back windshield. Doug's head lights up, but he doesn't move.

"Shit..." Tony mutters, covering his mouth.

"He's just drunk. That's what drunk people do, they pass out. We'll go open the doors and wake him up, then get moving."

"You're very calm about this, especially considering how you didn't really want to come out here."

"What can I say? I'll be taking my 'told you so' any time now," she beams, turning the flashlight upward at her own face to look like a demon.

They both step up to the car and grab a door handle. Sharon pulls hers and cracks the door ajar, causing Doug to immediately slump over. Tony stops himself from leaping over the car as Sharon stifles a shout. She flashes the light directly in Doug's face and he begins to stir.

"It wasn't me, officers, I just fell asleep," he slurs.

Doug and Sharon groan together in exasperation.

"We came back to get you, bozo," she grumbles. "Where did Madison go?"

"She had to go take a piss. She said she was going down by the water."

"Christ, Doug," Tony chastises. "You really let her go down there alone and with no light?"

"What's the difference?"

"The fisherman might drown her down there, that's what!" Sharon scolds him.

"You don't believe in all this? It's a myth! There's no silly fisherman or drowning bodies, those are just stories made up to occupy drunk teenagers. Hell, I was just trying to occupy a drunk ME."

"Hey, you guys made it back! Is the tire fixed?" Sharon turns quickly with the flashlight to see Madison stumbling up the hill.

"See?" Doug chuckles, "it was just a goofy story about a dumbass fisherman. Lighten up, Tony."

A harpoon bursts through the windshield and impales Doug's head against the back seat amidst the unmistakable sound of shattering glass. The steel bolt sticks straight out from between his eyes, and he instinctively reaches up to try and pull on it for several seconds with a blank face devoid of thought. Both his hands grasp for the rod aimlessly without ever actually grabbing it, before his body finally falls limp.

Sharon stands outside Doug's open door, getting pelted with renegade blood spatter as the squelch of his skull being invaded rings through all their ears. She holds still and in a state of shock.

Tony covers his mouth tightly and falls back on the ground, yet regains composure quickly and runs toward Sharon. He takes her hand and begins to dash back the way they came without even taking the time to wipe the blood from her face.

Madison stands frozen in panic, watching Doug's feeble attempts to remove the spear from his face. After a delay of several seconds, she brings her head back to unleash a mortified scream.

"Madison! We have to run now! Madison!" Sharon pleads to their catatonic friend.

A faintly visible figure in a yellow suit lumbers forward and raises the speargun again.

"Madison! Now!"

"Go! Turn and go, now!" Tony shouts, nearly lifting Sharon off the ground to pull her away.

The second shot rings throughout the trees and over the open plain. Sharon turns desperately to check on Madison as they run in the opposite direction, but all she sees is the harpoon projectile only a few feet from her body, seemingly stuck in stasis mid-air. One pump of the heart feels like a minute's worth, cascading through her body as though an avalanche of blood has burst her arteries open. Madison is as good as dead already, and there is nothing she can do about it.

The spear lunges forward in real-time, bursting through Madison's ear and exiting the other with roughly equal lengths protruding from both sides. She falls back limp and in the same dire shape as Doug.

"Sharon!" Tony's voice cuts through the fog. "Sharon! RIGHT NOW!" She realizes suddenly they have already begun to run away as her feet move involuntarily beneath, while her mind remains wishing she could have saved Madison. She always thought horror movie characters acted unpredictably, but it turns out watching your friend's murder feels like…nothing. An overload of the senses unlike anything she could ever be prepared for. The worst thing she had ever experienced to the power of ten, and that may be only scratching the surface of the horror her body is currently hiding beneath a galvanized surface.

They run. Cool night air burning their lungs and throat, yet they continue running onward, trying their damnedest to leave the atrocities behind and complete the impossible escape. Why did they return to the car? They were FREE, yet decided to voluntarily walk back into the lake of fire.

"We can get there, Sharon! I can see the street now! Go, go!"

A teenager steps into their path, looking decrepit even under the limited light of the moon. Tony hits the brakes and nearly spins out like a runaway car. Sharon stands beside him, feeling the pounding of his pulse inside her hand. The young girl tries to speak through garbled sounds as water pours from her mouth. Each syllable produces another mouthful of liquid falling to the ground. Their eyes adjust finally to find the girl's skin a pale shade of blue and her eyes a dull grey. She raises her left arm and points to the lake adjacent.

Tony turns to Sharon and nods decisively. He channels his best tackle from his college football days and barrels through the girl like a rabid bull, still grasping Sharon's hand for dear life behind. She feels a bit of warmth within just thinking about Tony's protective instincts, which consequently happen to be one of Sharon's favorite aspects of him. He would never leave her behind no matter how dire the circumstances, which is at least a small bit of comfort within the current situation.

Now three figures step before them, appearing to be a family, but Tony doesn't stop this time. He bowls through and immediately runs into resistance behind as more and more lifeless grey-blue faces step in to hold him back. He cocks his arm back to swing at the assailants, though their numbers overpower him and they easily take control of the skirmish by holding Tony's arms down.

Shadowy creatures circle overhead amongst the trees and ready to pounce. Scores of drowning victims surround Sharon and Tony to ensure they don't escape the lake. He grows restless in holding and elbows, claws, and wills his way to freedom while buried under the watch of an unrelenting army. They finally acquiesce as rows of them step aside in front of Tony to reveal the yellow-cloaked fisherman emerging from between the scattered sides of the dead.

Tony continues to swing, as is his nature, punching repeatedly those impervious to his punishment. More pile on in their stead, latching to limbs, necks, and heads, when eventually Tony and Sharon stand immobilized under the yellow-suited man's gaze. Sharon stares at her boyfriend for the final time, a man so sure and true, now held limp by characters of an urban legend.

The fisherman primes his speargun for the third time. Tony widens his eyes at the gravity of the situation and throws several more elbows in a frenzy to be free. The harpoon shoots through one of the drowned victims' chest and opens a wound from which water flows onto the ground. He drags

Sharon further but finds it as difficult as running out from a pit of quicksand while the legions of the drowned grasp at his shoulders again.

This is it. Sharon recognizes it, as do the damned. She quivers violently, grasping Tony's hand inside her own clammy palm while the yellow fisherman stares them down maliciously behind the darkness of the shadow cast by his hat. He turns and marches toward the lake, followed by the dead who fall in line. A shove from behind sets Tony in motion, still clinging to Sharon's hand. "What do we do?" she trembles.

"What can we do? They're pushing so hard, it's not even an option to stop. My other arm is being held down too."

"I'm scared, Tony. I-I don't even know what to say, you were right, we should have listened to you. We should have just gone home."

"Stop," he whispers. "There's nobody else I would rather die with. I just hoped it would be much later, but here it is."

"We accomplished it all, 'til death do us part," Sharon laughs through tears. The only sound to be heard is the synchronized stomping of the deceased trudging forward, their waterlogged shoes turning the trail to mud with each squish and step. A raven croaks somewhere overhead, it must be near sunrise now. "How are you not scared?"

"Of course, I'm scared. I wish there was something we could do, anything at all, but I think that option is gone. I'm all ears if you're working on a plan."

They begin to walk downhill and the glass-like surface of the lake enters their view with the sliver of moon reflecting at its center.

"There's power in a crescent moon, you know?"

Tony squeezes her hand and smiles weakly. He sees another group of the dead to his left and out of Sharon's view, dragging long, thick chains hooked into Doug and Madison. They tug his friends slowly and methodically into the lake, nearly without disrupting the surface. He keeps this to himself for Sharon's sake, or maybe for his? Can't be sure anymore.

The yellow fisherman wades into the water at about knee-level. He turns and stares at the row of drowned victims, who stomp into the ground even harder as they pick up the pace. They descend mindlessly into the bottomless lake in a single-file line, the sounds of footsteps decreasing progressively as more of them march below.

Sharon and Tony step into the water with trepidation as icy premonition rises through their shoes. This will be their tomb. The fisherman stands to the side of the line staring as the young couple wades further out for their baptism into the legend of the bottomless body of water, Lake Umbra.

They squeeze each other's hands one final time as they are forced further out and the tops of their heads bow beneath the surface. Bubbles arise for several seconds, until the final one pops and silence overtakes the land. The fisherman observes to assure nothing or nobody returns, then saunters out of the lake as the ravens begin to croak in earnest.

XXII
Killers Anonymous

"Good evening, ladies and gentlemen. My name is Chip and I am your secretary. I am also a recovering killer."

"Hello, Chip," rows of unenthusiastic audience members greet in return with a combined monotone.

"Before we begin, let us take a moment of silence for our fallen victims who could not join us today."

Groans roll through the rows of occupied folding chairs in their meeting hall. "Why would the victims be here anyway?" someone in the back comments.

"Well, Ronnie, they couldn't be here even if they wanted to and you know why? Because you murdered them, now pipe down and take a moment of silence." They all sit quietly and uncomfortably while Chip briefly lowers his head. "Fantastic, now we may begin for the evening. As many of you are aware, Killers Anonymous is a fellowship of men and women who share their experiences with each other in hopes that they may defeat a common enemy and help others to stop killing people before the electric chair calls your names. The only requirement to be here is a shared desire to put our pasts behind us and strive to be better versions of ourselves moving forward. Now that that's all over, would anyone wish to share? The floor is yours."

Chip walks across stage, past a whiteboard that says '3 weeks since last incident', and takes a seat in his chair.

A woman takes the stage with hesitation and accidently clears her throat directly into the microphone. She stares through the several rows of similarly-minded addicts in their dimly-lit meeting hall. "Hello, everyone. My name is Zoe and I'm…I'm a murderer."

"Hello, Zoe."

"Thank you. I have not killed in seventy-one days, though the urge has been overwhelming lately. I stare at each of you now and I…I would just DIE to slit your throats and peel your facial skin back over your skulls. No offense."

A few grunts, chuckles, and inquisitive remarks echo back.

"Anyway, pardon my manners. I just miss it so bad, you know? Nothing in life has any meaning anymore, it's like I'm searching everywhere just to find something that can fill that void. So far, nothing, but what I can promise to all of you tonight is I won't give up."

"That is incredibly brave, Zoe, thank you for speaking tonight!" Chip applauds from the other side of the stage.

"I feel better already! It is fair to say that nothing will ever compare to dismembering male prostitutes, but attending these meetings is helping me cope."

"You…what?" someone whispers from the front row.

"That was my *thing*, you know? I used to patrol for male prostitutes downtown and take them to hotels, remove their fingers one by one then move up to wrists, elbows, and shoulders. Seems a bit silly now that I haven't done it in so long."

Unenthused before, everyone in the audience is now leaning forward and enthralled in their seats with eyes open wide.

"Goodness, there wasn't a Saturday night that went by for what seems like years where I wasn't out driving the town and following hookers, trying to find…that special one. You all know what I mean, that feeling where you would rather kill yourself than not be able to kill that person."

Hearty agreement ricochets back at Zoe. The energy level in the room multiplies, causing Chip to break a bit of a sweat.

"Thanks, Zoe, that-"

"But I'm not done. Then I found THE ONE. His name was Raul, and he was the reason I feel compelled to kill still, the one I compare, or compared, each successive victim against. My muse, perhaps. Raul almost seemed to… enjoy? losing each one of his different-colored fingernails until he eventually lost consciousness. I kept reviving him as long as I could, but the little guy just couldn't hang after a certain point. Anyway, I've been chasing that thrill ever since."

"Tell us more, we need more!" Ronnie hollers from the back. Several others clap, while many of them just breathe heavily and rub their sweaty palms together. Zoe grins.

"No, thank you, Ronnie," Chip interrupts, dashing to the microphone. "Zoe has had a turn to speak and now we need to give others an opportunity before our rental time is up. Anybody else? A bit less…provocative?"

"I would like a turn," a twisted looking man lumbers to the stage.

"Fantastic, a newcomer! So nice of you to share tonight. Go on, the stage is yours." Chip returns to his seat adjacent.

"Hello, everyone. My name is Otis."

"Hi, Otis," they return.

Otis scrunches his face in discomfort at the booming, singular voice. "I have not murdered a human in over two hundred days."

Applause all around the hall.

"Congrats, friend! You've come to the right place," Chip encourages him.

"Thank you. However, I-I-I kill small animals every day. Right before I came here, I killed one."

"You…what?" Chip responds with gritted teeth as the crowd begins to turn. "Get him out of here! Get the FUCK out!" he shrieks as several massive men grab the kicking Otis and launch him out the front doors by the back of his shirt and belt like a scene from an old slapstick film. They all applaud once again as the stranger plops on the pavement.

"I am terribly sorry," Chip continues, "but…THAT will never be tolerated here. Who's next? Please, anyone who can cleanse the palette."

One hand raises from the precise center of the room. An inconspicuous looking man who had been there a time or two, yet never spoken until this evening.

"Yes, sir. Come on up."

The slightly undersized man stands and turns to his right methodically, walking in front of several killers with an air of nihilism in his step as if nothing in the world is of concern. Clear-framed glasses and a little boy's haircut adorning his head and face, even the largest and most hardened individuals in the room feel slightly inadequate in comparison.

"What's your name, friend?" Chip greets him.

"E.E. Erna."

"Hello, E.E.-"

"Save it."

The screech of a skidding car tears through their ranks. The sound of a pin dropping could be heard, if anyone were to dare drop one. The runt of the litter declaring himself alpha in front of capitulating participants, the body of sadism incarnate and chaos unbound taking center stage.

"I am a murderer and have been for as long as I can remember. I do not necessarily wish to deprive myself of this pleasure."

"Now, E.E., one of our primary rules is-"

He shoots Chip a vitriolic look that would kill a rattler in its tracks. Chip straightens his posture and stares straight ahead into the crowd.

"As I was saying, I do not wish to quit for the sake of it. Addiction is a burden I do not wish to succumb to, however. I have decided to cease as of yesterday, my last kill, and I reveled in every minute of it. She was a waitress, my final girl, if you will. I sat outside in the vehicle every night for three weeks, drinking my own black coffee and wishing she would be serving it to me as I observed through the glass diner windows. With binoculars I ascertained her name to be Roberta."

E.E. has grabbed the room by the throat. They wait for his signal to breathe, which is currently coming at a premium. They are already engrossed in his story and desire to kill, which is boiling over into the audience.

"I observed Roberta, the way she held her server's tray, the manner in which she passed out glasses of water. The way people smiled at her with genuine happiness, just happy to be in her presence. I couldn't stand it. I wanted to bash all of the backs of their heads with an iron club. Repugnant, obnoxious happiness, nothing I hate more. And to do it in public? Hate of the highest order, a display of despicable emotion for nothing more than a plate of eggs placed in front of them. PATHETIC!" he smashes the podium with both fists and laser-guided missiles for eyes.

Several attendees jump in the audience, startled by the outburst.

"Night after night I observed and DESPISED these people, but none more than her. Roberta. The bringer of joy with her infectious personality, I wanted her to suffer. I wanted her to pay for every bit of happiness and every smile she delivered, an equal and opposite reaction paid in full, and then some. Roberta, the name of rumination as I repeated it to myself ad nauseam alone in the car. I watched for weeks longer, salivating at the thought…the moment when I would finally end her life!"

Electricity jolts through the room as countless killers lean forward in their seats and listen with bated breath.

"Thank you, E.E., but we must be moving on now. My visitors share how they're coping with the stress, not about how great that stress was, you know?"

"Finish the story! What happened?" someone anonymous shouts.

"Give us more of that shit!" Ronnie echoes.

E.E. turns to the confidence-ridden Chip with a smirk and continues. "What, you want to know how I…killed her?"

"Yes…" nearly every onlooker recites in catatonic unison.

"You want to know what happened next?"

"Yes," they all nod in agreement.

"Stab me in the leg," one of the women whispers to her immediate neighbors.

"I lurked outside that diner for nineteen uneventful nights with my hands tied, waiting for the precise moment I would know to be right. It's a special feeling and unmistakable against anything else. Words cannot even BEGIN to describe, though I suppose I will try nonetheless. That final night, HER final night, she bounced out of the restaurant so overly pleased just to be herself. I nearly gagged. Nothing could have prepared me for what happened after that."

"Christ almighty, man! Tell us what happened!" Ronnie bellows, tense and sweating. Several others appear to be quite pale and unwell.

"Yes, we are just about to get there. Please stop prolonging my story with interruptions. So, she walked to her car, happy as can be. I watched vicariously...she reached for the handle and pulled it slowly, saddling herself in the front seat. Little did she know, nor any of you, I had been watching from her back seat each night before, pressed flat to the ground in secrecy. Eighteen evenings before, I rode to Roberta's house yet lost the enthusiasm necessary to follow her inside. Something about not seeing her serve people, no smiles on either side, neutered my desire to kill. She was boring alone, listening to the car radio in silence otherwise. No cheer, no happiness. Each night I lay hidden in darkness, yet lost the urge by the time we got to her house."

E.E. turns and glances at Chip, who is staring back in anticipation with both eyebrows raised, exactly where he should be.

"THIS NIGHT, however...I felt ready to blow like a stick of dyna-mite! So I leapt forward and attacked that charming bitch in the driver seat, pouncing on her as she yanked the wheel and tossed us both in a ditch!!!" E.E. explodes with energy after a night full of reservation. Most of the room gasps.

"Dangling upside down," he continues," I choked her unconscious and climbed out of the vehicle with my own forehead bleeding. Euphoric, I stifled howling laughter in favor of dropping to my knees and riding the vibrations of joy that the smiling woman would smile no longer!"

Cheers erupt as the tide of the room turns to anarchy.

"But my dear friend, dangling limp upside down inside her own crashed car, what was I to do with her? She might have died before someone found her, sure, but what kind of climax would that be? So I grabbed a piece of jagged glass and nearly sawed her fucking head off! Kill!!! Everything you see must fucking die!!!"

The front row springs from their seats and frothing at the mouth, leaping over their chairs and attacking the second row. Toby crushes Richard's windpipe, Damien stabs Mia in the ear, and Zoe beats several others to death with her chair.

"Stop! Stop it! You have all worked so hard on your recovery!" Chip screams. "You're ruining everything!"

E.E. smiles devilishly at the podium, observing the pendulum of chaos he set in motion. He watches as someone lays on the floor, flat on their back, while another places a chair leg in his mouth and jumps on it. He stares while Ronnie rushes the coffee pot and smashes the scalding liquid over his neighbor's face. Pandemonium and discordance everywhere, it makes him grin.

The members of the room rapidly drop of unnatural causes, from thirty-six down to twenty-two in a heartbeat. The bodies build mass in the center of the room between piles of tossed chairs, blood and fallen teeth decorating the scene like an abstract painting.

"What have you done?" Chip stares with pleading eyes. "God help us all."

"Just wait for what happens next," E.E. grins with a snarl as he checks his watch, then walks down the hallway toward the front door, flicking the lights off on his way out. "Hello, yes, I was the one who called you." The violence comes to a halt as every killer in the room listens intently.

"Yes, I own this building and we are pleased to host your city council meeting this evening," he continues. "I am sorry to hear that your regular building has no air conditioning, but I am sure you will be quite comfortable here. Please, walk down this hallway and I will get the lights behind us. That's it, just keep walking."

"Mr. Erna? We are in the room now, may we have the lights on, please?"

"Yes, of course." He flips the lights and immediately turns to pull a steel shutter across the exit, locking the prey in the room with the predators.

Blood-curdling shrieks and terrible screeches ripple through the confined space of this living nightmare as the townsfolk gaze upon the carnage strewn about. Shredded remains and blood puddles lay at the feet of those still standing, who salivate and stare at the trembling newcomers.

"Have at it," E.E. says to the crowd as he strolls by on his way back to the podium, "have a blast!"

Ronnie charges forward, but slips on a bloody hand and gets trampled by the ravenous survivors advancing. The city council members scatter, yet are trapped by the stampede flanking them from all sides. Zoe ambushes the mayor first and hacks him apart, then ravishes the mayor's aide standing directly behind. Toby bludgeons the secretary while someone else E.E. has never seen demolishes the mayor pro tempore with a broken mop handle. Several council members cower in wake of their impending fate, yet to no avail. The predators before them have been starved too long by the one who held the chains, Chip.

Damien, the largest of the bunch by a fair amount, lifts a body of slight-frame off the ground and uses it to beat the remaining council members to death, turning to threaten anyone else who would dare attack him from behind, swinging the corpse through the air and catching Barron in the head with the crack of thunder.

A sharp whistle pierces their ears. They turn to see E.E. standing proudly center stage, staring down at the body farm he propagated. "Listen up! Who here feels neutered? Because you are, and you have been for some time, you bunch of eunuchs!"

The man closest to the stage takes offense to the accusation and charges E.E., who cracks a smile so slight in the corner of his mouth, nobody in the room catches it. He pulls out a blade as the man leaps on stage and rapidly cuts a gash in his face from ear to ear. E.E. immediately pounces on the fallen assailant and rips out his esophagus with his teeth, standing with a grin and throwing the throat at the crowd.

"Any more of you…eunuch MOTHERFUCKERS have anything to say? NO?! You are the top of the food-chain, or at least you were! Until this tiny, pathetic man took the knife to you and clamped the chains on while you weren't looking," he turns to point sharply at Chip, hiding behind his chair. "My only question is…why? And how? How did three dozen godless murderers fall victim to his sweet-talk and nonsense and allow yourselves to be caged like misbehaving house pets? Absolutely revolting!"

"E.E.," Chip whispers from behind the chair, "I don't think you know what you're doing."

"Oh, I know exactly what I'm doing, CHIP. Why are you all killing each other? He's the one who pushed you to the edge of the cliff! Haven't you ever thought of killing him?"

"E.E.…."

"What kind of man strives for nothing more than to control others? And you're okay with that? Ronnie, I can see you breathing. Get up."

Ronnie hesitates and stands with a sigh, falling in line with his colleagues.

"Do you see how complacent you've become? Set yourselves free and kill this man! Take his life and toss him in with the rest of these sheep!"

The dozen still-living killers rally behind their de facto leader's speech and storm the stage with whatever violent objects they picked up along the way.

"Everyone, let's take a breather! Remember your steps! In your recovery, whenever you have been wrong you promptly admitted to it…now is one of those times! Who is this person that has been allowed to walk in here and take advantage of you? That's it, HE'S trying to control YOU!" Chip attempts desperately. "Ronnie! How many meetings have you been to now? You would have been swinging from a rope if not for me!"

Ronnie, Zoe, Damien, and the others continue forward maliciously with evil grins. Ronnie reaches the stage first and breaches Chip's safety wall.

"E.E.! Call them off! Ronnie!"

Nobody changes course. Zoe climbs on stage, then Damien, and then nine violent others with a mind on vengeance. Leading the pack, Ronnie holds a chain in his hand and turns to E.E. for approval.

"What are you looking at me for? You need my permission?"

Embarrassment compels Ronnie to swing his chain and strike Chip across the neck. Eleven others behind him accept the open invitation to strike their former mentor with broken glass, knives, screwdrivers, and the back of a chair. They slash, slice, and hack him apart like starved carnivores all trying to get a piece of forgotten livestock. Down goes the counselor in a ball of flames, killed by those he swore to save.

E.E. pulls a pistol out from the back of his waist band and blows a bullet through Ronnie's forehead, causing him to fall on top of Chip's deceased body. Ten more bullets rip through the air, and ten bodies hit the floor in a heaping dogpile on top of Ronnie. Zoe stares at E.E., visibly shaken yet still standing.

"Congratulations, Zoe, I have chosen you. That many killers living at the same time...ridiculous. You are free to go, in the most literal sense, and continue doing what you do best. Conquer."

"I'm free?" Zoe stammers.

"You are free. Carry on the tradition and be well, Zoe. May you live a life of freedom. Say it."

"I will live a life of freedom?"

"Good. Now go, enjoy it. You've earned this," E.E. acknowledges with a nod.

Zoe takes several quick steps away, but turns back before leaving. "Why, though? Why me?"

"Why not, Zoe…why not? You're alive and nobody else here is. Now go."

She sprints down the hallway without another word, before something else bizarre happens. Zoe had been one of the biggest believers in the program, her recovery, all of which are now ashen remnants floating in the rearview.

E.E. strolls across the stage and kicks Ronnie in the side of the head with a chuckle. He digs Chip out to lift him off the floor and plops him back in his chair with one leg crossed over the other and a hand placed judgmentally on his chin, staring down at the pile of bodies on-stage. The great hall, so recently vibrant and booming, is now quiet as the interior of a sealed coffin and E.E. much prefers the present company, as well.

He hops from the stage and carefully maneuvers one arm from each body to point accusingly at Chip. Surveying the room one final time with his arms folded, he nods in approval and hits one light switch to leave the room dim, but still visible for whoever should enter.

"This is my best one yet," he decries to nobody, then turns and walks proudly down the hallway.

XXIII
Hell is Other People

"Help me! Why is everyone ignoring me, somebody please help!"

Faceless strangers turn and stare without making an expression, not a single one of them in my time of need.

"What's wrong? Why are you so agitated, friend?"

My body convulses, yet doesn't move from its position. I look down at the harnesses strapping me against my chair. "What possibly could you mean? Do you not see the restraints placed upon me? Have you no sympathy that I am trapped against my will?"

The grey-faced minion sitting next to me turns and stares, blank like all the rest. "Hello, neighbor, but I do not see any such thing. You are as perfectly free as me."

I look down and the chains are gone, yet their weight lingers still. My breathing is labored and I feel that if I don't immediately run away, I will burst from within. I shake off the invisible shackles and leap from my seat to the dismay of many others in the vicinity.

"Pardon, but is there something you need? We do not allow people to walk around the airplane mid-flight without purpose. Please, either use the restroom or return to your seat."

"Can anyone explain what is happening? I never boarded an airplane! I don't want to be stuck here, somebody please let me out!" I feel my heart pound harder at the prospect of being trapped.

"Let you out where? The only option is down, though I'm afraid you might not survive the fall."

"How bad can it be to sit in your seat? Just relax and enjoy the ride," another says. They all look the same, no expression, no features. Just plain faces indecipherable from each other to my brain.

"I don't think any of you understand, I did not ask to be on this flight! I would like to be anywhere else in the world but here, and now one of you is telling me I have no choice?"

"You don't have a choice. Please, sit down like everyone else. Why are you being difficult? Stop being problematic, nobody else is."

I begrudgingly return to my seat with great reluctance and close my eyes. Seconds pass and I am unable to sit still any longer, feeling a rush of adrenaline that forces me upright. I look out the window for clarity and see nothing amiss in the eyes of the other passengers, which is to say there is only blue sky. Suddenly, the faint outlines of flames enter my vision, coming from one of the engines. I try my hardest to stifle the urge, but I leap involuntarily once again.

"We are going down! Somebody do something, the plane is going to crash!"

The faces stare, unwilling to budge, even if quick action could mean their survival.

"You need to relax, that's all."

"But we are all going to die, don't you understand? Why doesn't any-body care? The plane is on fire!"

"I do not see anything," one passenger claims.

"There is no fire, you need to calm down," another recites.

The airplane IS on fire, and I AM going to die. There is no escape from this vessel which I was forced upon. This is a nightmare. An unequivocal, inescapable, living nightmare.

"You seem tense. Would you like something to pacify you?" the pas-senger next to me offers.

"No, that won't extinguish the fire or release me from this plane. I am going to die and nobody cares. You're all going to die too, so have fun with that."

"I can help you off this airplane, that is simple."

"You can?!"

"Yes. Just...don't want off and then you are free," my neighbor blinks blankly.

"You call that advice?! Just don't want off to get off the airplane?"

"Yes. That is the only way out. I am on a secluded island right now and it is magnificent. You want it too badly, stop wanting off the plane and you will get it. Relax."

Not the worst advice I have ever heard, though the harder I try to visualize myself free on solid ground, the more I feel trapped. Where do I wish to be? I'm not even sure anymore, I am out of happy places hidden up my sleeves. Perhaps I should try closing my eyes again and think of some-thing else.

The passenger next to me, my neighbor, touches my hand on the arm-rest. I do not mind entirely, though it briefly disrupts my quest for peace. Ignore it, I repeat to myself, ignore the feeling though it is all you can feel.

Your every emotion focused on this hand touching yours…ignore it. Ignore it, though the more you wish yourself to do so, the more this hand burns a hole into yours.

I open my eyes at last to see my neighbor fully aflame and feeling the heat carrying over into my chair. "Help, I am going to burn to death! Somebody put this fire out!"

"There is no fire, I do not understand why you are not relaxed yet?"

But there must be a fire, because I feel the pain on my own arm and travelling upwards. I am burning to death, I can feel the excruciating pain. I am going to die because nobody around will lend a hand.

The person sitting in the seat beside me, the one overtaken by fire, turns to face me with a relaxed expression not unlike the rest of the passengers. "You create your own problems. Everything is fine until you let yourself think about it. You need to stop doing that."

Well, what does that mean? The fire is gone now, though the agony of burnt flesh lingers. All I want is to escape myself, but even if I could, I would still be stuck within this metal tube. I leap to my feet and wish to claw myself free, but the vision from the window shows we are headed straight down into the ground. The massive airbus we are all riding has taken a negative vertical descent without anyone noticing, but me, of course.

"The plane is going down! We are about to crash directly into the ground!" I sit in my assigned seat for as long as I can before the urge for freedom grows too strong. "We are going down now, so let me out! Please, let me jump from the plane instead of perish inside. Let me die free!"

One person from the row in front of me stands and rotates slowly to stare. Another creaks upward, then another. Eventually, each row rises and turns to gaze directly at me with sunken black eyes and blurred features. I look around to see there isn't a single passenger sitting anymore. Every expressionless face is peering within my soul as I stand and make a scene, exposed and emotionally nude. Their gape burns within.

"I said the plane is nearly crashing and we need to do something! All anyone has done since I've been on this plane is ignore my warnings! You strapped me to my chair, trapped me on this plane, stared at me when the engine caught fire, and now sit there like a bunch of invalids as I shout we are all going to die! You may not care, but I do!"

"But you're not on an airplane," the child directly in front of me says, "you are at home safe in your own bed."

"What?! I can see you saying that to me! How can I be anywhere else but in the middle of all these people? We are all going to die...I have to run for help," I warn, yet my feet refuse to move, cemented to the floor. The restraints spring from my seat again and wrap around my chest as I fight and resist with every bit of strength left. "No! What are you doing? I'm the only one who can help us!"

"There was never a fire, until you showed up."

"The plane was perfectly fine, until you caused it not to be."

"Everywhere you go, hell follows."

I feel like I am sinking into a black hole below quicksand inside my chair. They are blaming ME? "But..."

"You always do this wherever you go."

"It's always the same with you, disaster and catastrophe while the rest of us are at peace."

"You really aren't comfortable until your world is burning, are you?"

"I...but there IS disaster and catastrophe...my world is about to be burning when we crash..." I reply weakly, severely doubting my disposition.

The child in front of me rounds the row of seats and plops down beside me in a chair that is suddenly empty. "It's okay. You do this a lot, but it will be alright. You are in your bedroom right now, lying in bed."

"But I am sitting on a plane! How can I be at home?"

"I know, try to relax. If I *told* you that you're dying, would you still believe it then? You are in danger, everything is bad, this is the end. Is that what you want to hear?"

"No, I don't WANT to hear that," I answer. "It just seems to usually be the case."

"Because you ignore every other outcome. I need you to snap out of this delusion and return to where you belong. You always manufacture your worst fears, do you know that? Are you aware?" the child speaks with an elder's wisdom.

"I...I can't breathe...please stop, my chest feels tight..."

"Don't you see? You are impervious to the horrors of the world but be wary of the mind, for it can be more deceiving than anything or anyone else. It's funny, your walls are so high, yet you don't even realize the enemy has already breached them."

"Can you explain what you mean?"

"You already know. Wake up."

The inside of the metal tube coffin dissolves into my bedroom, exactly as the child warned. Safety. Comfort. How could I have found myself in such a morbid predicament? Perhaps I will lay here for a moment longer and reflect, recover.

What happened? I don't remember the sequence of events leading up to my imprisonment on that plane. What a horrible thing that was! My worst fears come to life as if by design. Being a claustrophobic is tough, although the only thing that could have made it worse...

My mind wanders and I find myself back on the airplane, shackled to the chair and near death again, with a strap of tape over my mouth to make breathing that much more difficult. All things considered, I have been in this situation before and can relax in the lack of unknown. I shout beneath the tape and every plane passenger turns to stare at me once again, only now they are...CLOWNS?

XXIV
The Truth About Cannibalism

"**B**ugger, I've been shat on by a bloody bird! We're rolling? Hello all ye faithful, it is your humble narrator, Oliver Walker come to join you again with our new special, 'The Truth About Cannibalism'. This week we're on location in the wop-wops from an undisclosed location off the coast of our native New Zealand. The mission? To meet with a local cannibal society and prove to you they are more mate than foe. We will be back with you shortly once we make way into the island."

"Okay, cut."

"Cameras off?"

"Yes. Or, cut," Peter, the cameraman confirms.

"It's rank out here, innit? I'm already knackered and we've only just started."

"You're doing great, babe. Remember how important this trip is to end the injustices against lifestyles alternative to ours," Olivia, Oliver's wife, reassures him.

"Yeah, I know it. I'm here, aren't I? Just let me smoke a durrie before we go tramping through the jungle."

Peter rolls his eyes but pulls out a smoke of his own.

"Don't take too long, Oliver, I'm excited as! I think I'll have myself a lolly to snack on in the meantime. Can you believe it? All the years of planning and we finally made it here. This is going to change the world!"

Oliver and Peter exhale smoke and nod.

"These poor people, they've been maligned for so long, eh?" she continues. "Now we will be able to share that they're PEOPLE like you and me, only with different preferences."

"You couldn't be more right, Olivia. Think of the ratings!" Oliver enthuses.

"Don't be an egg, Oliver, it's about more than viewership! This is an opportunity to make a difference! This is why we got started in this business, or don't you remember?"

"Yes, babe. I do remember, thank you for reminding me. Peter, have a piece of chuddy."

Peter reaches for a stick and nods. "At least our breath won't smell as bad as this island."

"Your breath is better, but you still smell scodey, mate. Let's have at it then?"

"Yes, let's!" Olivia agrees, jumping up from her temporary rock.

"Peter, I think you should roll cameras the entire time from here on out. That way we don't miss anything for the documentary, eh?"

"Yes, but can you keep your comments to yourself, then?"

"We'll edit that out."

"We're live, we can't edit that out."

"Alright, everyone, Oliver returning!" he snaps back into character. "Here with my lovely wife, Olivia and making our way into the jungle. Say hi, babe."

"Hello," she waves with great enthusiasm. "We'll be with our guests in a jiffy, but have a squiz at the beautiful and curious sights around while we walk!"

"Cut?" Peter suggests.

"Don't cut, damnit, we just started rolling!" Oliver shouts. "Just speed this part up or something."

"It doesn't…we're LIVE, mate."

"We aren't actually that far, babe."

"Bugger, fine. Just get us another minute or so then cut and we can pick up again when we get there."

"Helloooo, Oliver here again!"

"And Olivia! We have arrived outside of the Kai Tangata society, and there are heaps of things to show you today. The Kai Tangata are a rich and storied people whose culture deserves immense praise. The irony is they have lived just off the coast of New Zealand all along! Our neighbors, in fact."

"Right you are, Olivia, our neighbors, but not the kind to come and ask you for sugar! These lovely people feast only on the finest of delicacies which many of us have never come close to trying; human flesh!"

"I know what you're thinking, gross, disgusting, revolting even. But this island suffered a great famine in the 1970s and the inhabitants ate everything else that moved or grew, later adapting to survive and hunt each other for a feed instead. This shows incredible resourcefulness I only wish I was capable of."

Peter pans the camera around the island to showcase the beautiful green shrubbery. A member of the Kai Tangata stands about ten paces behind Olivia and Oliver.

"Oi, Gizza geez! We've found one! Look at him, in all his majesty. He's a friendly bugger as would be expected from such a beautiful society. Hello, cuz!" Oliver greets.

The tribesman steps forward, as do Oliver and Olivia. They are now dangerously close to meeting face to face. "Cuz," he repeats.

"Cuz, eh, we're mates already!" Oliver exclaims, laughing. "Aye, cuz, we are friends come to help out. Please, take us to your village to meet with your leader."

"Cuz," the Kai Tangata repeats.

"Cuz, aye. Please, take us to your leader. Ahem, rangatira? Yes? The bossman or woman?"

"Rangatira," he nods, turning to walk away.

"Eh? You wish for us to follow?" Olivia repeats rhetorically.

"Rangatira."

"This is fantastic, friends. We have touched down in Kai Tangata territory as friends and have been welcomed into their village," she continues. "Today we make the first step in repairing a centuries-long prejudice against our brothers and sisters!"

"Join us as we deliver you an exclusive inside look into this closed society, so stay tuned, you will only find this type of content right here on Walker TV," Oliver continues.

"Is that a cut?"

"Don't you bloody dare, Peter," Oliver warns. "I will eat your face off me self."

The Kai Tangata turns to ensure the three videographers are still following as they enter a narrow pass which secludes their village from the shores of the island. Only someone incredibly knowledgeable, or a fool, would find and walk along this path covered by foliage.

"Hey, bro? Have you got a name for us to call you?" Olivia questions.

The man turns and scowls, then continues his march without missing a beat.

"Alrighty then! Fair enough. Friends out there, for your information, the Kai Tangata are an intensely private group and we are extremely privileged to have even been invited this far. Please do not attempt this yourselves, as we have dedicated years to studying their ways and customs."

"And it's all for you, our viewers! You're the ones who make this all happen, so stay tuned for what's in store!" Oliver adds on.

"Oi, take a geez up there!" Peter exclaims as they exit the tight path and enter a lush valley full of vegetation.

"It's mint! Couldn't have asked for better," Olivia gushes.

"Olivia, babe, I thought you said there was a famine on the island and they only eat humans out of necessity?"

"Yeah? And?"

"Well, it's just that I see at least a dozen edible plants growing here, that's all. I just wonder why they don't eat them instead?" Oliver wonders.

"Oh, babe, don't pack a sulk! We're here, just enjoy the experience!"

The Kai Tangata guide releases a guttural bellow as the four of them enter the sacred valley. Several others exit their homes as he greets his people in a dialect foreign to Olivia, Oliver, and Peter.

"Absolutely mint!" Olivia whispers yet shouts into the camera lens. "Here we get to observe the gathering of an entire culture before us, which the outside world has never been witness to. The Kai Tangata have a strong societal structure, which eh…well it isn't immediately apparent who is who, but we will figure that out! Peter, focus on that man and woman there while we move in."

"Right-o."

"Oliver, move in. Make contact."

"Yes, babe. You take point."

Olivia and Oliver approach slowly toward the center of the crowd. Oliver seeks approval on his position with Olivia, who nods reassuringly for him to step forward.

"Ahem, greetings! My name is Oliver and we come to your society in peace!"

"Babe, I don't think they know English."

"Right. Erm…kia ora, mates!"

Everyone standing around erupts into hearty laughter.

"Ha…ha ha! Olivia, I think they're buying it!" Oliver laughs along.

"Keep at it, Oliver, look! One of them is approaching you."

A young and slender male figure steps forward from the crowd and places a hand on Oliver's shoulder.

"Babe…babe! I think he likes me! You getting this, Peter?"

"You already know I am, ay."

"Good, keep it rolling, keep it rolling. Kia ora, friend. Nice to meet you."

The young man, shirtless, rubs his hand over the shoulders of Oliver's jacket.

"Look at him! I think he wants your jumper, babe. You should give it to him!"

"Yeah? Alrighty then! Go on, mate. Have it," Oliver says, removing his jacket and handing it over. "Bit warm out here for me anyway."

The young man takes the jumper and puts it on inside-out then turns toward his people and poses. They all laugh again while he mimics Peter.

"Go on, mate, enjoy the moment. What more can I say, you look munted."

He returns with a grin and proudly wearing his jacket, reaching for Oliver's shorts and giving them a tug.

"You can't have me stubbies, cuz! What will I wear then?"

The young man's disposition changes to something between a mix of serious and offended. He tugs Oliver's shorts again.

"Take them off, Oliver. You don't need them," Olivia advises.

Oliver feels his face burning as he drops his trousers in front of an entire village. The young man grabs them and pulls them up his own legs, now wearing Oliver's entire outfit. The Kai Tangata laugh again, not at the nudity, but at their brother dancing in a foreigner's clothes.

"What do you propose I do now, Olivia?" he asks, standing in nothing but his grundies and an old off-white undershirt.

"Be calm. You have made friends with them, now hold it."

"Yes, dear," Oliver replies apprehensively, sweating bullets. He slowly turns his head to make sure Peter has the camera fixed directly on them, but sees two renegade Kai Tangata standing behind him with what looks like femur bones in hand. One of them clocks Peter across the head, while the other catches him from falling and rips into his ear.

"Fuckin' hell, Peter's carked it! Run, Olivia!"

Olivia turns to look at Peter falling to the ground, followed by both his assailants diving onto him and shredding his throat. She immediately notices the camera falling to the ground and hopes it's still recording, even though Peter looks like he's covered in T-sauce and clearly gone.

"Olivia! Run! Get out of here before you end up a feed, yourself!" Oliver's voice shatters her dream-state as the young man wearing his clothes pounces and bites into his outstretched forearm. Several others rush and claw into Oliver's meaty torso, followed by most of the village, who carry him off to the barbecue pit.

Olivia snaps to attention and sprints for the hills where they came. The two cannibals who took down Peter have joined the crowd in transporting Oliver, so she runs for his body and recovers the still running camera. She dashes for an indentation hidden in the mountainside and turns the lens toward herself.

"Olivia here. Our team has faced some unfortunate adversity thus far, but the mission will prevail, and that is to demonstrate to the world the Kai Tangata people are much more than simply mindless monsters. Please, observe." She pokes out of hiding and zooms the camera into the concentration of the village, where they are all gathered around Peter. A man enters frame with a large blade and systematically cuts him into delectable chunks of meat for the village to cook.

"Alright then, bad example, ay? Fear not, faithful viewers, I will finish what we came here to do, even if that means putting my money where my mouth is!"

Olivia silently rounds a corner to be within full view of the villagers, yet they are too pre-occupied with Peter to notice. The young man wearing Oliver's clothing chews on Peter's hand like a dog with bone, covering the jumper in a spray of blood.

"No worries, everyone, just looks like a bit of T-sauce, ay? She'll be right, then, let's carry on. Peter, he's a goner no matter how you slice it, no pun intended. No more harm done." She places the camera down on a flat rock for a moment and pulls a silver flask from her fanny-pack. "Might as well be on the piss before this one, ay?"

The Kai Tangata begin to chant ceremoniously down at the base of the hill.

"That's my cue," she speaks to the viewers, zipping her flask away and sprinting with the camera under one arm before sliding into position behind a hut. Their party has already begun, which is the moment they will be most joyful, and therefore the most vulnerable for Olivia to make her mark.

"Hello, friends! Please excuse my lack of manners. Kia ora!" Olivia announces, filming the reactions of the villagers before propping the camera on what appears to be a table. "My name is Olivia, and I am your mate even though you are currently eating one of mine. I forgive you! Yeah, nah, scratch that, there is nothing to forgive."

Every man, woman, and child has stopped what they are doing to gawk at Olivia, many of them either cooking or chewing pieces of Peter. One male steps forward excitedly after seeing their new friend approach. He continues slowly with a malicious grin before increasing into a full run toward Olivia.

A gunshot bowls them over with an echo through the small village ground. The advancing boy crumples with a perfectly-placed bullet hole in his forehead while Olivia holds the smoking revolver to a round of gasps. One of the elders holds a hand up to hold them all in place.

"Alright, you bunch of knobs, listen up! There are plenty more bullets where that came from in me bum-bag. You see me standing here? Yeah? Mate," she pokes herself in the chest, "cuz, friend. I am on your side, if you allow me to be."

SYMPOSIUM OF THE REAPER: VOLUME 2

Two men exit one of the huts with a long wooden pole resting on each of their right shoulders. Oliver sits affixed between them in a traditional pig-roast with an apple in his mouth. They march toward the burning fire and prop their dinner above it.

"Oliver…" Olivia whispers, tears filling her eyes. "You would be so proud to know you will feed an entire society tonight. Bless you."

"Psst. Psssssst. You, girl." The young man wearing Oliver's clothes murmurs to Olivia while the tribe is distracted by the pig roast.

"You speak English?"

"Yes, I do. There are a few of us here that got stranded for whatever reason."

"Explain to them what I said!" she whisper-shouts. "Tell them I'm a friend of the cause, I support the tribe, whatever you have to do!"

"There's no need. They don't eat women, in fact they worship you."

"Then how did you come to join them? Why didn't they eat you?"

"No meat," he relinquishes. "They said I was unappetizing. Grotty. I proved my worth and they allowed me to join. It's quite nice here, actually, I rather enjoy my time. Plus, it's not like I have a ute hidden to drive away", he chuckles.

"Right. What's it going to be, then? Tell me what I have to do to prove myself, eat Oliver?"

"No, of course not. You must eat your victim. Raw. His life may be replaced with yours, but only if you combine spiritually. You will then be one of us for life, forced to adapt to the way of life adopted here."

The elder steps forward with a hatchet and hands it to Olivia, bowing his head. She initially hesitates, then buries it deep into her victim's chest and pulls out his heart, holding it up in the air for the hollering and adoring new fans. Her people.

XXV

The Beast and Me

Here we go again. I don't necessarily agree with his actions, though I get it. At the end of the day, it's a living.

I am excited to leave the house again, however that usually means only one thing. Think positively, Jake. You never know, this time could be different, though to my memory, which admittedly doesn't tend to span very long, it has never been different. The end result is always the same.

"Come on, Jake! Let's go, hop in the front seat!"

I would love to, yet the thoughts of what we are going to do alternate between dread and excitement. I love riding in the car! But I don't want to go…if only these decisions were more direct. Car it is. Tillman shuts the door behind me, rusty hinges creaking as the heavy steel door closes with force.

Car rides are my favorite. What comes next is a close second, but this is the best part. I wish we didn't have to, but Tillman takes good care of me and I don't see any other way. I sure am hungry, though. A full belly usually helps mitigate the guilt.

"You ready, Jake?"

I sure am. It's been a while this time, maybe longer than any gap before. I'm starved. He opens my door again and I make the long leap down. Tillman towers over me as I walk alongside him, partners in crime. My tail wags involuntarily a few times along the way.

A young woman approaches in the distance. It's dark out here and I can smell her apprehension as she looks at him, yet she softens…once looking at me. She is disarmed and continues walking forward. This is typical.

"That is such a cute dog! May I pet him? And what is his name?" the young woman asks as we meet on the sidewalk. My tail wags again.

"Of course! His name is Jake and he is a good boy."

That makes one of us.

"Yes, he is! Hi, Jake," the woman greets cheerfully with her lips pursed, scratching behind my ears. That's my cue.

I dart down a dark alley suddenly as if chasing a rat. I can hear them faintly behind me continuing in my footsteps, pretending to be interested in my concerns, though I know the drill. This poor girl won't be alive within the hour. Darkness descends, yet I continue further onward.

"Is Jake alright? He's running awfully far."

Yes, very far, far away from the street where we could be seen. We have been here before and I can still smell my tracks. Her tracks.

"He's quite independent, aren't you, Jake? That's it, good boy, show us what you're after!"

I'm a good boy. I'm doing a good thing for my human. The end of my tail wags slightly, even though I try my hardest to stop it. He's proud of me and I am doing a good job. I turn to face them and sit down with both ears perked up and tongue dangling. One small bark should get her attention.

"What is it, Jake? He's so funny," the woman laughs. "Why did you bring us all this way?"

Look cute, Jake. Wag your tail and pant harder, they always think that's a smile. I'm excited and can't help but pat my right paw on the grimy ground as she walks closer with her hand outstretched to pet me. Yes, that feels excellent.

The sound of a wet crunch hits my sensitive ears followed by several more of the same. Tillman's shadowed outline towers over her, even from behind, as her face goes from joy to pale shock. She drops to her knees as he stabs her several more times with the precision of a surgeon, yet brutal nonetheless. My left ear drops and my head cocks to the right. This part never pleases me, particularly when they are as friendly as this one, but what comes next...

"Good boy, Jake. You're the only one I need in this world."

No, not that, even though it's life's highest calling. Tillman trusts me implicitly after I have proven myself time and time again. The real treat comes later when we get home, after he loads the girl up in the truck, gets me in the front seat again and drives us home. We're in the spare bedroom now and she lays on the table. Tillman raises a butcher knife high and brings it down on her wrist, then tosses the hand in front of me.

Finally, my gift, the spoils of war. My mother's side, that being my wolf half, burns with desire staring at the flesh bestowed upon me. The call of the wild to eat what you technically killed replaces my rationality, my father's side, while staring at her hand on the floor. I leap onto it and eat every piece in only a couple crunchy bites. Tillman stares down proudly as the hand is thoroughly consumed, then tosses me the forearm.

Life's greatest pleasure, a delicious meal of fresh meat. Yes, she was very nice, though feeding my wild instincts trumps having my ears scratched. I eat the forearm bone clean, then run it outside while he prepares more pieces for me to eat. Once I have had my fill, Tillman will dispose of the rest as it starts to spoil and becomes inedible, even for me. It's a wonderful life.

Sometimes he goes places without me, which I don't mind because it allows me time to rest and live the life of a normal dog. Sleep, play outside, lick my paws. I suppose Tillman is much the same way; in between killings he is largely an unassuming man who likes to lounge and not do very much, at least not around me. Then he begins to grows restless, impatient, going from pacified to agitated at the drop of a hat. I know my time to perform draws near again, though I do not get fed much during the down time. He has to keep me motivated, he says.

Every now and then the thought crosses my mind while he is sleeping on the couch…if my hunger becomes too much, I can just eat him while he sleeps? No, no, that would be bad…be patient. It will make the next meal that much sweeter to wait for it. I'm a good boy, I repeat to myself often. My human tells me so.

This particular time he seems unmotivated to continue. It has been a long time since the last one, or so my stomach tells me. My afternoon leisure time in the yard becomes hunting season for squirrels, cats, and birds. Primal instincts overtake again to satisfy the need in the pit of my stomach which can't be filled by tiny bowls of compressed powder called dog food.

Finally, the day comes, after a more prolonged time period than I have ever been forced to wait before. Tillman opens the passenger door to his truck and invites me inside. My tail wags with force and the impatience I suffered through suddenly feels like a forgotten memory. The pinnacle of life and I couldn't be happier. He climbs in the driver seat and off we go. I pant so hard looking outside, the window fogs up and I can't see anything else. Happiness.

Today, we travel to a different type of place I have never been before. There are people all over, which already sets my fur on edge, but even stranger, they all have a dog on a rope standing next to them. This is a nightmare!

Tillman circles around the truck toward my side as he has done countless times before, and pulls my door open. This time though, he has a rope in his hand too, with a circle attached to the end of it. He tries to loop it over my head, but I do not like it at all…pulling my ears back until they touch and stifling a low growl, I give him my best indication that I do NOT want this to happen.

"Don't do this to me now, Jake, god damnit, let's go! Put it on!"

This is…an issue. I'm a good boy, after all, but one that cannot be confined. Nor should I be. However, I can't remember a time when Tillman has ever let me down, so with great reluctance and against my best judgement, I lower my guard and allow myself to be chained. I've been a wolfdog a long time, my entire life in fact, and have never felt so silly as I do now, that is… until we enter the grassy area and my stomach rumbles staring at the dogs' humans. Wonderful meat in all directions and the reason we must be here. Faith slightly restored.

"There you go, Jake. That's much better, let's go get you some dinner. You would like that, wouldn't you? Wouldn't you, Jake?"

I cannot help it, and I wish it didn't happen, but the thought starts my tail wagging. Great, he probably thinks I *like* the rope around my neck.

"That's right, good boy. Remember, I need you. None of this happens without you, Jake."

He needs me. Okay, I can do this, especially if there is a fresh meal at the end of the road. Tillman walks toward the crowd and eventually pulls the rope tight, yanking me forward by the neck. I have never done this before. He tugs several more times until I start moving and join him at his side. Many other smaller dogs stare at me judgingly, though little do they know I would rip their throats out if I wasn't on a special assignment. I march on proudly, ignoring their glares with my chest held broad. A low and deep growl as we pass is enough to silence all their thoughts.

"Jake, stop it. We're here for the girl, not the dogs. Behave," he whispers sharply.

Behave. Tillman has killed men before too, but women are usually much more receptive to the canine, or lupine, companion. Oddly enough, there are mostly women here today with their dogs, so just about anyone around could be the target and not one of their dogs are built to protect them.

What's this? Two of the smaller dogs approach to introduce themselves. No! Away with you! I shoo them silently, but they don't leave, in fact they seem far too comfortable. I lob and hurl insults and threats, yet they only wag their curled-up tails and stand blankly like empty cups without a thought of their own. One of the owners is abrupt and yanks her dog's rope back to pull it away from me, but the other…that must be her. Tonight's meal.

She has brown hair and a smile that stretches across the entirety of her face, already a sign of bad things to come for her. Youngish, maybe thirty, though the human species makes almost no sense to me. At this point, she has lost all interest in her own dog and is instead fixated on me, another indication Tillman has already sunk his mental claws into her. I must repeat again, but I do not enjoy what follows; I only make the best out of the situation I've been placed in. Tillman is who he is with or without me.

"Your dog is beautiful! What breed is he? And what's his name?" the woman asks.

"Thank you. His name is Jake and he's actually half wolf."

She yanks her hand back as if touching something sharp. "A wolf?! He isn't going to bite me, is he?"

Tillman looks down at me and plasters on a smile only I know to be fake. He's good at this.

"Of course not! I wouldn't bring him here around all these other dogs if he wasn't a good boy."

The woman leans in again, though I sense reluctance, I can smell it. My first instinct is to bite clean through her fingers for a snack, though that would ruin my meal in more ways than one. I can't help but sniff her hand as it approaches, being that it smells like other dogs. Curiosity wins.

"You're right, he is a good boy." She continues to scratch behind my ears while her pathetic dog watches in jealousy.

"Of course, he is. So, what's your name, anyway?"

Extended seconds of silence lapse between them as she stares at Tillman.

"What, you're not going to tell me?" he counters stiffly.

"Isn't it funny how we grow up our whole lives afraid to give personal information to strangers, then as soon as we're adults we hand it out like candy?"

They stare at each other for an uncomfortable silence once again. He looks down at me and I wish I could shrug in return.

"I'm kidding, lighten up. My name is Victoria. You seem harmless anyway," she winks at him. Oh, how I wish I could shrug at her now. Tillman only grunts in return.

"Well? What's your name, or are you afraid I might stalk you?"

"It's Tillman, I'm Tillman."

"That's an interesting name," Victoria answers. "Can't say I've ever met a Tillman, though you look like one. Is that a first or a last name?"

There's my sign. He hates when people grow too interested in his personal life, so this is where I step in and bark at her dog, who nearly has a heart attack.

"Knock your shit off, Jake," he scolds with a yank on my chain, knowing full well what I did for him.

"Oh, he's fine! He probably just wants to play, don't you, Jake?"

No. I want to eat your hand waving in my face.

"Go ahead and say hi, Jake, it's okay!" she continues. "This is Frankie. Say hi to him, Frankie! Don't be afraid!"

I don't much like Frankie in general, but Tillman gently nudges me and I never break character when put to the task. The small and shivering dog cowers beneath my approaching snout. Just let me sniff you and I'll be done for both our benefits. Quite unpleasant. Frankie isn't winning me over.

"There we go, Jake. I have a way with dogs, do you know that? I suppose you wouldn't, but now you do. It is something of a gift, though not one I can share physically. May I?" she asks Tillman, gesturing toward me.

"Sure," he deadpans.

Victoria cups both hands under my snout and raises my head to meet her eyes. What a bizarre human, usually they are dull as can be. Now she is whispering and I would like to bite her.

"No, you don't want to bite me."

My ears shoot back and a surge rushes through me. Take your hands off me, I don't like this anymore.

"Calm, Jake. Calm down and look at me. Just look at me." She rubs beneath my ear with two fingers and continues to stare. Okay, I'm listening.

Her eyes speak a thousand words, yet say nothing at all. This is both weird and enthralling, warming even, and I find myself growing slightly fond of her. I can smell her suddenly in the best way, perfume overloading my senses. I feel...comfort.

Tillman yanks the chain slightly to break my concentration. "Time to go."

"Oh, I didn't realize...I mean, if you have to leave, that's fine."

"We do. Nice to meet you."

Victoria and Frankie scurry off awkwardly. I glare at Tillman, thinking with my stomach and feeling disappointed that a meal got away so easily. He pauses for several seconds, then holds up her wallet.

"I snagged it while she was talking to you. Let's go, we'll meet her at home." He reaches down and finally removes the chain. My tail wags.

We march back to our car to escape before Victoria realizes what happened. One of the passersby stops with a small dog of her own.

"You know your dog is supposed to be on a leash? What kind of dog even is that?"

"Fuck off," Tillman counters, marching on. A man of singular focus with his eyes set squarely on the target. He sure is great.

"You must be starving, boy. Me too. Just in a different way."

We sit in the truck now down the street from Victoria's house. Night has fallen over us while we wait. Tillman stares out the windshield, unnervingly still and calm, so I do too. Dinner is coming.

Without saying another word, not that he does often, he opens the car door and circles to his left. My tail does the thing again where it wags on its own and I have no control over it. The day has been long and stressful with an empty and grumbling belly, but we have nearly made it to the finish line. My door swings open now and it's go-time. Always trust the process.

The neighborhood is dark and the houses are spaced-out well, almost perfect for the type of evening staring us down. To the outsider, we are a man and his dog walking down a desolate sidewalk, yet only we know the truth. Victoria was nice, though I'm starved and not thinking like myself. Tillman stops in his tracks, so I take a nice drink from the gently running gutter water in preparation.

"Okay, Jake, this is the house. I'll let you through the backyard gate and you know what to do from there."

I don't, although I have an idea. Run to the sliding door and growl lightly to get the dog's attention. Frankie...? Then bark loud and uncontrollably until both of them exit the house, distract and divide. Tillman slips in through the door as Victoria inspects the yard.

"Jake?! Is that you? What are you doing here?"

I know I shouldn't, but I like her energy. Shaking my head, I snap back to the present moment and bark once more to grasp her attention, then dart past and run inside hoping they give chase. Nice house, Victoria. The first thing I'm going to do as I wait is eat all Frankie's food.

She must have been settling in for the evening when we interrupted, as only the living room light and television are on. Otherwise the house is dark and ready to get gruesome. My senses are overwhelmed by the smell of Victoria on every surface, which makes sense inside her own house, but the magnitude is dizzying. It feels like she is surrounding me from every side, rushing into my nose and filling my head with intrusive thoughts of her. This is incredibly confusing in the wake of previously wanting her for dinner. I feel...fondness for her.

"Jake? What's wrong, are you in trouble?" She walks toward me from the door with concern in her face.

Before I can bark 'no, but you are', Tillman shakes the floor with his heavy run from the dark kitchen. The sudden commotion startles Victoria and she blindly swings a baseball bat hidden at her far side hidden in the shadows. The wooden barrel strikes Tillman's jaw, but the momentum carries his massive frame forward and tackles her to the ground, smashing her head on the coffee table.

They both lay still in the aftermath of the attack, although he continued stumbling a bit further than she did before hitting the floor. Frankie barks uncontrollably in retaliation, but is easily fixed with a deep, rumbling growl in return. He flees from the house to leave his human defenseless and alone, an embarrassment of the highest order. I don't know what to do to help them, I don't even have thumbs, but I would NEVER run away.

Victoria stirs first and without a sound, though I sense it loud enough. She lays still for a moment under my observation, trying to keep her breathing quiet, yet she shakes. "Jake…"

I hope she doesn't mean me?

"I need you to help me, Jake. Come over here so I can see you, good boy. Please."

WHAT?! My ears perk straight up, as does the hair along my back. Good…boy? She thinks I'm a good boy too? I wish I could help her, but then what does that mean for Tillman?

"That is a very bad man that has raised you, but I know better, I SAW it earlier when we met. Don't you remember, Jake? I could tell you know right from wrong, even with that evil monster pulling you by the chain."

That damn chain, but he did it for my own good. He was trying to find me a meal, which led me to you. And I am happy he did. My tail wags as I stare at Victoria, even though she doesn't appear to be awake, laying still on the hardwood. She is doing a great job pretending.

"I can tell you care about me, don't you? Then help me. Attack your master, kill him, eat him. I know you've thought about it before."

But how did you know that? I have, though it is painful to admit. I just get so hungry when he doesn't feed me…

"You have to choose, Jake. You can only rescue one of us, so who is it going to be? This is not a good lifestyle, but I can take care of you. I can feed you every night, love you and keep you safe. You can stop living like a wolf and become a dog here. How does that sound? All you have to do is kill that man before he wakes up and then you're free. Chew his face off so I can take care of you, because you know I will never be safe if he is alive."

Kill...Tillman?

"Kill Tillman, yes, you have to. It won't be hard, he is only laying there just like I am. But hurry! He might wake up any second now."

A normal life. I thought my life *was* normal, or at least by our standards. Now I'm staring down the barrel of a life without Tillman, the only human I have ever followed, to join the magnetic Victoria. I look over at his unconscious body and wonder for a second if this will be the last time I ever see him? Could it really be the end of the road? No. He's my beast.

I leap through the air, wolf in the driver's seat, landing on her body and tearing it to pieces. Finally, a decent meal and a full belly. Tail wagging, I trot over to Tillman and lick his face to show him how we did. My human, the monster I am responsible for.

XXVI

Satan Claus

"Don't you ever just get off your phone?" Matt chastises while everyone in the circle stares in agreement.

"Oh, I'm sorry. You must have forgotten what it's like to be in a relationship since it's been such a long time," John defends himself.

"No, he's right, we set this trip up weeks ago," Chad piles on.

"Come on, John. This is a guy's weekend," Christian slurs, already deep into their alcohol supply.

"Put it away, bro," Nick piles on, lobbing a marshmallow over the campfire at John's head.

"You know what? Fuck you guys, I'm going to go get another drink and let you have a little boy time, okay?" John stands and wanders off into the night while his friends laugh at him.

"Who invited him?" Jesse speaks finally, sitting on his own while the rest of the chairs are placed in a semi-circle on the opposite side of the fire. "Anyway. Back to my story, the legend of Satan Claus."

"It's a stupid story anyway," Chad interrupts, always the skeptic and first to kill everyone's buzz. "It's just a myth based on a demon named Andras."

"Shut up, Chad, let him finish," Christian blurts out drunkenly.

"Who is Andras?" Nick asks.

"As I was SAYING, Andras is a demon who possesses humans and uses them as puppets to kill other people."

"Satan Claus was real, alright? He used to kill people every year around Christmas time," Matt argues.

"Satan Claus isn't a person, it's a curse," Jesse continues. "Everyone who listens to the entire story will be unsanctified and targeted by the entity."

"Oh no, we're fucked now, guys!" Nick mocks to a round of laughter from the semi-circle while Jesse sits stoic.

"Satan Claus will leave gifts for all of us, though some say the presents are empty and simply meant to scare us, while others say the gifts contain the curse of possession. There is another group, however, that believes we will all die in random accidents after opening the boxes. Nobody has ever seen Satan Claus and lived."

Christian, Nick, and Matt look around at each other uncomfortably.

"Then where do the stories come from?" Chad cuts the tension.

"I thought you said he isn't a person?" Matt interrupts before Jesse has a chance to answer Chad.

"He's not a person, it's an embodiment. Now shut the hell up and let me finish the story."

"What's an embodiment?" Nick asks.

John returns to his seat directly perpendicular to Jesse. "Are you talking about all that satanic shit again, man? Get out of here with that."

"Hopefully he's coming for John first. He relies upon the telling of this story to thrive and keep his legacy alive. It is difficult to say whether he is a murderer or if the deaths were truly accidents, from inexplicable car crashes to falling icicles."

John rubs his eyes, exasperated while Chad sits next to him staring incredulously.

"One man was burned alive inside his own house, where mysteriously none of the doors would open once the flames began. Satan Claus takes whatever he needs from each person to accomplish his objective and then moves on to the next. His end goal is to kill humans, and nothing less."

Christian accidentally burns his marshmallow in the fire, listening to the tale with disgust. The rest of his friends sit still yet in distress.

"Now that you've heard the whole story, you can run for the rest of your lives and never escape. You will never be free, and never defeat the demon, or human, or whatever Satan Claus is."

Jesse completes his story and relaxes back into his chair, satisfied at a job well done. The bonfire flares outward, nearly reaching everyone sitting around it as they all exclaim.

"You almost burned me, man!" Christian shouts, scooping his charred marshmallow from the floor.

"Thanks for the fairytale." Chad sits unamused and sipping from a flask.

John, Christian, Matt, and Nick goof around, discussing the story and making jokes. Christian makes an obscene gesture to Satan Claus and John pretends to push him into the fire. Levity and jocularity are had by all on their annual December friend trip with a large fire and good drinks, all except for

Chad and Jesse, who doesn't say another word though none of them notice due to their excessive alcohol consumption.

"You know guys, it IS Christmas time and that serial killer was never caught. He could be watching us right now, out in the middle of nowhere," Matt muses, getting the group back on topic.

"What was his name again?" Nick asks.

"The Mistletoe Murderer."

"What kind of a dumbass name is that? And how do you even remember something so stupid?" Christian gripes, throwing his empty beer bottle at the fire.

"I don't know, man. I'm just really interested by things like this."

Eventually the good times slow and they put the fire out, returning to their tents for the night while also preparing to return home in the morning.

"Chad. Chad? Chad!"

"What? What?!"

"What's your deal, bro? I thought you learned your lesson with the drugs, man," Christian pokes.

"Nothing, just daydreaming. Tired."

Christian and Chad, the longest standing friendship of the bunch, also happen to be neighbors and drove to the campsite together, as they do every year.

"You know, obviously I don't believe any of it, but…I just keep thinking about Jesse's story. I don't know," Chad continues, massaging his eyes and deep in thought.

"Are you...are you really fucking with me right now? You, of all people, scared of a little ghost story? Don't you watch horror movies to fall asleep?"

"Forget it, never mind. He was just...he was so convincing is all and...I don't know, just forget I mentioned it. So, Christmas Eve dinner tonight."

Christian removes his hand from the steering wheel and looks over at Chad, lowering his sunglasses. "You know I'll be there," he grins.

"I just need to go grab a few more things before the stores start closing soon. Give me a few hours and I'll be ready."

Christian pulls the car in front of Chad's house and emphatically puts it in park. "You sure everything is alright, Chad?"

"Never been better." He opens the door and lumbers out of the car. "See you tonight." Chad closes it and begins to walk up his driveway before turning back and opening the door again. "Don't forget the drinks."

Christmas Eve morning turns to afternoon and then night, while their trip fades quickly in the metaphorical rearview mirror. Christmas lights and decorations flick on around the neighborhood as bitter cold falls upon their town, while the entire mood of the day changes.

Chad returns home from running his errands and unlocks the door to find a house sitting in pitch black. He immediately tries the light switch to no avail, yet notices the tree lights are lit and shining even brighter in the dark house.

"How the hell is the tree still on?" he speaks to himself without putting much effort into the thought. It rings through the quiet house as a reminder of the lack of company until dinner is ready. He remembers the flashlight still in his pocket from the camping trip, a safety measure necessary to survive in the middle of the winter woods.

Chad shines the light around his house, but sees nothing amiss. He walks toward the tree to inspect the lights and understand why they're still running, when he lights up a mysterious white and red gift that was not there earlier. White paper with red painted symbols which immediately cause him to grimace; inverted crosses and odd-looking stars and shapes of the occult. Chad sits on the floor next to the unwelcome present to think for a moment, ultimately pulling out his phone and dialing Christian.

Already diving into his glass, Christian sets it down to answer the phone. "Yo, what's up?"

"What the hell is this?"

"What is what, Chad? What are you talking about?"

"You know what I'm talking about, you're the only one who could have done this, you or Jesse. I don't find this funny."

"Chill, bro. It was probably just Jesse playing a prank. You know how he is, you remember the fire exploding," Christian speaks calmly to bring Chad back down to Earth.

"Then you got one too? So, it wasn't you?"

"Yeah, man, it was just an empty box. Relax!"

"It was empty?" Chad asks, skeptical.

"You worry too much, Chad, that's your problem. It's just a joke, you need to learn to laugh at it. Relax, have some fun. I'll come over and give you a hand, alright? Be there in a bit."

Chad hangs up the phone without another word, exasperated after a busy day and still needing to cook dinner.

Christian stares at his phone for a second and decides to call Jesse for clarification. A signal rings through the room that the line has been disconnected. "Okay, don't answer your phone, then," he speaks to himself, unbothered.

Chad sits in his living room and picks up the strange gift. The red paint is fashioned to look like blood running down the sides of the box, with tiny red 'ho ho ho' glittery stickers adorning the paper. He wrinkles his nose at the idea, but decides to unwrap the gift and move on with his night.

"Let's try giving Annie a call," Christian speaks aloud in his room. A long dial tone rings before she finally picks up.

"What do you want, Christian? Jesse's not here."

"Well, MY BAD. I just had a question for him, but he's not answering his phone. Sorry for assuming he would be with you."

"Oh, your friend, Jesse? That broke ass left me last week and never came back. We thought something was wrong at first because he left everything here. You really should choose your friends better," Annie patronizes through the phone.

Christian feels a punch in his chest. "I'm sorry, Annie. I didn't know. We went on our Christmas trip this weekend and…well, he didn't mention anything."

"He really didn't even mention me?!"

"Wait, you said he disappeared? He was just with us last night, so nothing could be…wrong?"

"He was acting really weird, quiet, not talking to anybody. Then he just disappeared and left me like the asshole he is."

He lowers the phone from his ear in disbelief, replaying the previous night in his mind and deep in thought.

"Christian! Are you still there?" she shouts.

"I'm sorry, Annie, but I have to go. I need to find Jesse right now."

"Oh, fantastic. Just like your friend, use me to get what you need-"

Christian hangs up and leaps from the bed without noticing the candle lit on his desk extinguishes on its own.

Chad pulls out a pocketknife and cuts along the top of his grotesque gift, peeling the sides apart and removing a black metal cross, inverted as he pulls it out and lit only by the red and green lights on the tree. He turns the cold steel over in his hands, bewildered. There is something else small in the bottom of the box, perhaps an object that might explain the idea of the prank. Chad reaches inside then hesitates for a second before ultimately deciding to grab the other item. A popping sound hits his ears first, followed by a projectile stream of blood into his nose and mouth as he gasps for breath, alone and kneeling before the tree. The velvety red liquid drips from his chin onto the floor while voices circulate the room and chant in his ears. The puddle reflects both an owl and Chad's face staring into it, urging him to rub the blood onto his forehead and eyes. So he does.

"You have reached the voicemail box of Matt. Please leave a message-"

"Someone needs to answer their damn phone!" Christian uncharacteristically loses his cool while frantically dialing everyone else that sat around the campfire.

"You have reached the voicemail box of Nick. Please leave-"

"Okay, God damnit. Answer!"

Christian paces the room for clarity and attempts to convince himself this is a massive misunderstanding, though he knows the truth. He ultimately decides to call Chad again and give in to his fears. The phone rings multiple times and seems to be another dead-end, when there is a click followed by shallow and quiet breathing.

"Chad! Thank God you answered, Chad, I think I made a huge mistake! I tried getting ahold of Jesse, but couldn't, so then I called John, Matt, and Nick and got their voicemail...can you hear me alright? Don't open the box, Chad! I said, DO NOT OPEN THE BOX!"

The creak of a wooden stair reverberates through an empty house outside Christian's bedroom door. He slowly turns his head to see the doorknob move silently at quarter turns, opening the door into the dark hallway to reveal a broad shadow.

"Chad?"

The figure lurches forward, unrecognizable with blacked-out eyes and deep bags beneath them. Christian's heightened senses compel him to leap off the bed, though his only exit is blocked. He desperately tries to run toward the corner of his bedroom as Chad lunges forward with inhuman speed and wraps a massive hand around the back of Christian's neck, yanking him backward as he panics.

Chad uses his other hand to grasp Christian by the throat and slam him down on the bed, leaning his full weight onto his longtime best friend's neck. The color begins to drain from Christian's face and vision, staring up at the exoskeleton of Chad with desperate eyes and knowing he failed, they all did.

Savagery consumes him and Chad cannot control the impulses of the entity within, digging his nails into the fragile throat crushing between his hands. Just as Christian's consciousness nears its end, Chad punches him repeatedly in the head and face before ultimately yanking his neck to one side and leaving it limply dangling off the edge of the bed.

"Imagine being part of something bigger than yourself. Bigger than your friends, your family. Giving yourself over to it entirely. What if you didn't have a choice but to serve? You may have to be bent and broken into submission... but you will lose."

Chad speaks ominously to a fresh group around a campfire, revolving his head around them one by one and staring into each set of eyes intently.

"He is unseen...and undetectable until your worthless existence is far beyond saving. They call him...Satan Claus."

The fire erupts upward and nearly burns everyone sitting around it. Chad leans back, satisfied his oath has been completed.